FAT MAN

IN A

FUR COAT

and Other Bear Stories

FAT MAN
IN A
FUR COAT

and Other Bear Stories

Collected and retold by

ALVIN SCHWARTZ

Illustrated by

DAVID CHRISTIANA

A Sunburst Book

Farrar, Straus and Giroux

"Uncle Lemmie Rassles a Stranger" is adapted from an untitled story in *Lumberjack* by Stephen W. Meader, with the permission of Harcourt Brace Jovanovich, Inc.; Copyright 1934 by Harcourt Brace Jovanovich, Inc.; renewed © 1962 by Stephen Meader. "Don't Rile Him None" is adapted from *No Room for Bears* by Frank Dufresne by permission of the author's agent Harold Ober Associates; Copyright © 1965 by Frank Dufresne. "Frank Clark Kills Old Ephraim" is adapted from "The Killing of Old Ephraim" by Frank Clark, *Utah Fish and Game Bulletin*, Sept. 1952, with permission of the *Utah Fish and Game Bulletin*. "Star Breast" is adapted from "Pablo Romero Roped a Bear" in *I'll Tell You a Tale: An Anthology* by J. Frank Dobie, with permission of Little, Brown and Company; Copyright © 1931, 1959 by J. Frank Dobie. "Sasha" is adapted from *Elephants in the Living Room, Bears in the Canoe* by Earl and Liz Hammond, with permission of the authors; Copyright © 1977 by Earl and Liz Hammond. "Big As a Cow" is adapted from "Bear Hunt in Reverse" in *Bundle of Troubles and Other Tarheel Tales*, edited by W. C. Hendricks, with permission of the Duke University Press; Copyright 1943 by the Duke University Press.

Library of Congress Cataloging in Publication Data
Schwartz, Alvin, 1927–
    Fat man in a fur coat, and other bear stories.
    Bibliography: p. 158
    Contents: Bear tracks—Strange encounters—Natural
enemies—[etc.]
    1. Bears—Juvenile literature. [1. Bears]
I. Christiana, David, ill.   II. Title.
QL795.B4S39   1984   599.74'446   84–4161

To Peter

Contents

BEAR TRACKS

A hundred years ago and more, a great many bears roamed the woods and the mountains. As one result, there were a great many bear stories to tell.

Pioneer families used to entertain one another with these stories. So did hunters, farmers, ranchers, cowboys, Indians, and others who had run-ins with bears. They would sit around a fire and tell their experiences. Sometimes they bragged or exaggerated a little, but that was expected.

Many of their stories were tales of high adventure. They set out to hunt a bear and fought it to the death, at times in hand-to-hand combat. Or they pursued giant "outlaw" bears that stole their livestock and could not be stopped. Or they rescued others from attacks by bears.

To outsiders, some of the stories seemed unbelievable. It was told that a bear knocked a hunter to the ground, then threw him across a horse, then got on the horse and rode away. It was said that there were bears that kidnapped human

children and raised them. It was said that there were also bears that understood humans when they spoke.

Of course, bears are no ordinary animals. They are among the most powerful on earth and among the most intelligent. When we see them in a cage, we forget how splendid they are when they run free. For thousands of years, they dominated life wherever they lived. With their great strength and speed, they were almost impossible to defeat.

Indians in North America learned this, to their sorrow. With only primitive spears and arrows as weapons, without horses on which to attack or flee, they were at the mercy of bears. Bears kept them from growing crops, raided their stores of food, and threatened their lives.

As humans developed better weapons, they gained the upper hand against bears, but that has happened only in the past two hundred years.

Something else sets bears apart from other animals. At times they look and behave like humans. They eat the same food we eat. They raise their children in similar ways. They walk upright on their hind legs as we do. They leave tracks that look like our tracks, except that theirs are larger.

They seem to think and understand as we do. As a bear shuffles along, peering this way and that, often it seems more like a fat man in a fur coat than it does a bear. And when that bear is shot and screams in pain, it sounds like a human crying out. There are hunters who have heard that cry and have never hunted again.

It is no wonder that many people think of the bear as a special animal. To Indians, Eskimos, and other northern peoples, the bear is sacred. They pray to it for protection and long life.

Many other people also have feelings of respect and affection for the bear, but these are mixed feelings. From stories they have read and movies they have seen, they have come to think of the bear as a friendly animal, as something like Gentle Ben or Smokey the Bear or bears that "Grizzly" Adams tamed. Yet they also know that a bear might kill one of them for no reason.

The last run-in I had with a bear was in Yellowstone National Park in Wyoming. I was asleep at the time, however, and so were my two young sons.

During the night, a large animal awakened my wife. She could hear it breathing as it moved around outside, sniffing here and there, circling our tent again and again.

While the rest of us slept, she lay in her sleeping bag holding her breath, hoping that the animal would not break in. After what seemed like hours, it finally moved away.

When she told us about this the next morning, we all thought she was fooling. "It sounded like a great big bear," she said, "maybe a grizzly."

"It was just a bad dream," I said.

But outside, there was a circle of bear tracks around the tent, and they were grizzly bear tracks.

STRANGE ENCOUNTERS

Frontiersmen in the American West reported seeing as many as twenty or thirty bears in a single day. Even as wilderness areas were settled, bears continued to be part of everyday life. They raided farms and ranches for livestock and other food. They wandered into small towns, and even invaded houses. In some places, schoolboys earned extra money by sounding an alert when they saw a bear coming.

Although there are not as many bears today, hunters and campers still encounter quite a few. Now and then a bear even turns up in the suburbs, as we shall see.

In the Dead of Night

THE TWO MEN made camp at the end of a long, narrow valley. One was a man from the East who wanted to learn more about Montana. The other was his Indian guide. It was 1896. One night the Easterner learned more than he may have bargained for.

"We had been hunting on this mountain for several days," the Easterner later wrote. "But we had found no game, not even tracks.

"My Indian guide said he would go up among the high peaks at the head of the valley and see what he could find there. He took a light pack with him and my big Winchester rifle. I stayed in camp to look after the provisions and the horses.

"In the dead of night the horses came down from where they were feeding and awakened me. I wondered why they had left their feeding grounds—whether something had frightened them—and went out from our tent to drive them back.

"After they had gone, there was a strange stillness. The night air was so cold, I quickly went back to my warm blankets, but I could not sleep. I had a feeling that something was near. I raised up and listened. Suddenly a rattling of pans came from the outdoor kitchen. 'One of the horses has come back,' I thought. I seized a stick and went out again to investigate.

"A huge shadowy form stood against the black line of the forest. But this animal was no horse. It gazed steadily at me with a lowered head that moved slowly from side to side. Then came a sudden snort, a sort of snarling whine. I realized that it was a huge grizzly bear, and I felt weak in the knees.

"I remembered hearing that it was certain death to run from a grizzly. So I put on a bold front and backed slowly into the tent. Then I started to build a fire. I thought the light might drive him off. But I was so frightened, it seemed like ages before I could find the matches.

"Soon after I had a fire burning, I heard the bear's footsteps. He was coming toward the tent, but he stopped near the door to look at my saddle. He stood there sniffing and grunting. Then he walked around to the other side. He raised himself up on his hind legs and rested his front paws on the tent poles.

"Where I was standing in the tent was directly underneath him. As the canvas pressed toward me, I could hear his heavy breathing. It was like a nightmare. I shouted at him, but my voice sounded strange and faraway. Then he dropped to all fours and went back to the outdoor kitchen.

"I watched him from the tent. He knocked the cover from a mess of trout. He ate a bowl of peaches. He tore open bags of flour and sugar. He found the heavy iron kettle I used for making bread. Inside, I had stored a great delicacy—a piece of butter. For a minute the lid on the kettle held fast. Then he struck the kettle such a blow that the lid flew off, and he licked up the butter. At the first sign of dawn, he disappeared into the forest."

Face to Face

In the spring of 1823, Jedediah Smith, the explorer and fur trapper, headed west with a small party of trappers from Fort Kiowa, South Dakota. They worked their way through the Black Hills to one of the forks of the Cheyenne River. There they came upon a grizzly bear. A trapper named James Clyman kept this record of what happened.

"We were leading our pack horses through a thicket when a large grizzly came down the valley. As Captain Smith came out of the thicket, he and the bear met face to face.

"The grizzly did not hesitate a moment. He sprung on the captain, took him by the head, and cut him badly. He threw him sprawling to the earth. Then he grabbed at his middle, broke several of his ribs, and ran off.

"None of us had any surgical knowledge. So I asked the captain what was best. 'One or two should go for water,' he said, and 'if you have a needle and thread, get it out and sew up my wounds.'

"I got a pair of scissors and cut off his hair. Then I began my first job of dressing wounds. I found that the bear had taken off nearly all of his scalp and had almost torn off one of his ears.

"Although there was nothing to stop the pain, I stitched the captain's head according to his directions. Then I told him I could do nothing for the ear.

" 'Oh, you must try to stitch it up in some way or other,' he said.

"I put in my needle, stitching it through and through, over and over, laying the parts together as nice as I could.

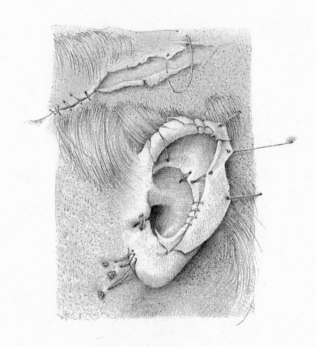

"Then the captain mounted his horse and rode to camp. We pitched a tent for him there and made him as comfortable as possible."

In time Jed Smith recovered from these wounds. He had come as close to being killed by a bear as he could without having it happen. It took an attack by Comanche Indians to kill him eight years later.

A Pot of Beans

WHEN JOHN COWLES and his wife and baby moved to Wisconsin in 1843, they built a one-room cabin to live in. All the cabin needed was a front door. That was due to arrive before the weather turned cold. Until then they had hung a heavy quilt over the doorway.

John Cowles was a doctor. One night just before supper, a messenger came for him. Someone was sick on a farm about twelve miles away. "I'll be home tonight or tomorrow morning," he told his wife. He quickly packed his things and rode off into the darkness.

His wife left a pot of beans simmering on the hearth in case he was hungry when he got home. Then she got into bed with her baby and went to sleep.

Sometime during the night, Mrs. Cowles awakened. She sensed that someone was in the cabin with her, probably her husband. But when she opened her eyes, she saw a bear in front of the fireplace. He was eating the beans, mouthful after mouthful.

Suddenly he stopped. He looked up and stared across the room at her. In the darkness, his eyes looked like burning coals. She wondered if he could see her. If the baby cried out, what would he do? If he attacked, what could she do?

The bear turned back to the beans. When he finished with them, he pushed the quilt aside and left.

Uncle Lemmie
Rassles a Stranger

UNCLE LEMMIE WAS A BIG MAN. He weighed two hundred and fifty pounds, mostly muscle. He could lift a horse. Used to do it for a bet.

Well, one frosty night in Vermont in the spring of the year, he was walking home from a dance, full of strength and cider. The road lay through the big woods, and there wasn't much moon to see by. He'd got within a mile of home when he saw a big fella in a fur coat sitting out in the road in front of him.

"Get up!" hollers Lemmie. "Want to freeze to death?"

The other one grunts sort of scornful. Lemmie didn't like the tone of his voice. So he heaves a big clod of dirt at him—catches him right in the belly. "Woof!" says the big fella and gets to his feet, waving his arms like he wants to rassle. Of course, rassling was Lemmie's specialty. "All right," Lemmie yells. "Come on!"

So Lemmie grabs him around the body, and, oh my, what a chest that fella had. Terrible strong in the arms too, and rough. First thing Lemmie knew, he felt fingernails digging right through his jacket. Then the earlap of his cap got chawed off. Lemmie had only been feeling playful. Now he got mad.

"Hey!" he hollers. "That ain't no way to fight! If you want trouble, I'll give it to you!" So Lemmie tries to trip him, but the big fella was too stout in the legs and wouldn't go down. Then Lemmie takes a deep breath and starts squeezin' him with his arms.

The fella snorts and twists, but Lemmie bends him way back, keeps huggin' him tighter and tighter all the time. Lemmie's chin is over the other fella's shoulder, so he can't see his face. But he keeps wondering who he is, where such a powerful man come from.

After a while, he feels the other fella's wind beginning to go out of him. Lemmie squeezes harder. All of a sudden he goes limp and falls down with Lemmie on top of him.

"Give up?" Lemmie asks.

No answer.

"All right," says he. "We'll stay here till you do."

About sunup, a neighbor came by. There was Lemmie asleep on top of a dead bear.

"Don't Rile Him None"

PETE PEEHAN BROUGHT the father and his fourteen-year-old son to the island in his salmon troller. While they were in Alaska, they wanted to go duck hunting. When the three rowed ashore, they found on the beach the fresh tracks of one of the big brown bears that lived there.

But Pete didn't see any need to worry. It was well into the fall, and the bears were beginning to den up for winter. "Not likely you'll be running into that one," he said. "But if you do, stand clear and don't rile him none."

Then Pete went down the beach to dig clams for supper. The boy and his father went off in the other direction to hunt ducks, the same direction the bear had taken. But the bear's tracks soon went into the woods. The boy and his father were headed for a shallow pool on the tideflats.

The pool was hidden in a thicket of tall beach grass. It was crowded with the ducks and other birds that fed there. When they were about two hundred yards from the pool, they stopped while the boy loaded his gun. His father sat on a tree stump and watched. When the boy reached the thicket of beach grass, he dropped to his knees and started crawling toward the birds.

As the boy's father remembered it, this is what happened next:

"All was quiet. Nothing had disturbed the birds, nothing at all—not even the brown bear that came silently out of the woods and waded into the pool.

"For a moment, I couldn't believe my eyes. Then I found myself out in the open waving my hat and hollering at the top of my voice. But there was no response. The bear, with its huge head underwater, was grabbing at salmon. And the boy was worming his way through the grass—toward the bear. Neither the boy nor the bear saw me or heard me. It was like a horrible dream.

"I started running toward the boy, yelling as I ran. But I already was too late. The bear rose up out of the pool clenching a salmon in its teeth. Then the boy stood up and looked into the face of the bear.

"At that moment the birds in the pool took off. The boy and the bear were caught in the confusion of a thousand pairs of thrashing wings.

"By the time the last bird cleared the pool, I had raced close enough to get the bear's attention. It dropped to all fours and came toward me. Out of the corner of my eye, I saw the boy aim his gun at the bear. The birdshot it fired would only send him into a rage.

" 'No! No!' I yelled. 'Don't shoot! Start backing away slow!'

"At the sound of my voice, the bear gave me all of his attention. I already had decided not to fire at him until he came a lot closer. But I didn't like the odds, and I started backing away. I expected him to charge at me at any time.

"But all he did was keep pace with me until he got to the lower end of the pool. There he stood and watched as we backed away from his private fishing hole. Then he went back to the head of the pool. He picked up the salmon he had dropped and vanished into the woods."

Rich, Warm Milk

ON A FRIGID WINTER'S NIGHT, a woman went out to her barn to get milk for her hungry baby. There had not been much for the child to eat that winter, nor for any of them.

As she crossed the yard, the wind blew out her lantern. But she knew her way, and on she went into the big, dark barn. Counting her steps, she found the stall where they kept the cow. She pulled up a stool and started milking her.

She hadn't expected much milk, for the cow was hungry, too, but there was plenty of it. She also was surprised by how low the cow seemed to be standing and how thick her coat was.

When the animal rubbed her furry head against the woman, she suddenly realized that she was milking a big she-bear. The bear didn't mind. She was glad to have somebody empty her aching udders. As for the woman, she kept on milking. She said later that her baby just loved all that rich, warm milk.

A Day of Mourning

A BOY NAMED MICHAEL HENRY lived in Yardville, a town just outside Trenton, New Jersey. On a warm night in June 1980, Michael was out riding around on his bicycle. At about ten o'clock he decided to go home.

"As I pulled into the driveway, I saw it," he said later. "But I couldn't believe my eyes. At first I thought it was a dog. But when I got closer, I realized what it was."

What Michael saw was a young black bear standing on its hind legs. It was not what one expected to see in a driveway in the suburbs. In all of New Jersey, there probably were no more than twenty-five or thirty bears at that time.

A policeman lived across the street, and Michael ran over to get his help, but he was on duty. His wife called police headquarters and told them about the bear. Then Michael went outside for another look. By then the bear had gotten into the garbage cans behind Michael's house.

"In a few minutes the cops came flyin' in like crazy," he said. They went into the back yard with a shotgun and quickly fired three shots. Then they came down the driveway, dragging the body of the dead bear behind them. It was not a big bear. It was five feet long and weighed about one hundred and fifty pounds.

Many people were upset by the killing. The bear was doing no harm, they said. It could have injured somebody, maybe killed them, the police said.

It should have been taken back to the woods where it belonged, people said. There was no time for that, the police replied.

Hundreds of people wrote letters complaining about what had happened. Some marched up and down in front of police headquarters carrying stuffed bears and big signs. "GRIZZLY ADAMS IS GOING TO GET YOU!" one of the signs said. There was even a day of mourning for the bear. People all over the area drove with their headlights on in his memory.

He Decided to
Go Down Fighting

BEFORE SUPPER ONE NIGHT, Sam Jessup discovered that he was out of potatoes. So he walked through the woods to a neighbor's house to borrow some.

On his way home in the dark, lugging a sack of potatoes, Sam made out a bear down the trail. He did not have a gun or a knife with him, or anything else to protect himself. Yet there was no point in running, for the bear would easily catch him. He almost could feel its claws and its teeth tearing into him.

Sam was so scared, he started to tremble. Then he decided he would attack the bear. Since he could not escape, at least he could go down fighting. He put the potatoes down, and rooted around and found an old tree limb.

Holding it like a club, he walked slowly down the path toward the bear. When he got close enough, he raised the club above his head and brought it down as hard as he could on the bear's head. But the bear did not move an inch. Then Sam saw that it was only a stump.

NATURAL ENEMIES

Now and then a large bear hunting for food may kill a small bear. Or a pack of wolves or wild dogs may kill a bear. Or some other powerful animal may do so. But it does not happen very often, for a bear is usually the strongest and the most intelligent animal where it lives.

There is only one creature that regards the bear as its prey and regularly hunts it. That is the human being. Humans are a bear's only natural enemies. Were it not for them, most bears would die of old age.

The Bear in the Sky

A BEAR AWAKENS from its winter sleep and leaves its den in search of food. At about the same time, a band of hunters leave their camp in search of something to eat.

This is how an old Indian legend about hunting a bear begins. It was told on a clear night when the stars could be seen, for it is in the night sky that this bear hunt takes place.

To see this hunt, you first must find two groups of stars. One is the constellation Northern Crown. It is a small half circle of stars. In this story, it is the den of the bear.

The other group of stars is the Big Dipper. You will find it in the constellation Ursa Major, the Great Bear. The four stars that make up the cup of the dipper are the bear in this story. The three stars that make up the handle of the dipper are the hunters.

As the seasons change, and the stars change their positions, the story unfolds. Often it was told in the spring, when the bear leaves its den. But it also can be told in other seasons, when one can see more of the hunt.

In the spring, a bear awakens from its winter sleep. It comes down the mountain from its den to find something to eat. Three hunters are also searching for food. In the distance, they see the bear and pursue it.

All summer long, the hunters chase the bear, but again and again, the bear manages to escape.

Late in the fall, the hunters finally overtake the bear. It rears up on its hind legs and prepares to defend itself. But the hunters quickly kill it, and it falls over on its back. They take the meat and bear skin and go on their way. Only the bear's skeleton remains.

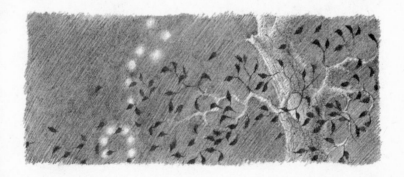

All winter long, the bear's skeleton lies in the forest, but its life spirit has gone. It has entered the body of a newborn bear still asleep in its den. In the spring, that bear will awaken and begin its search for food. At the same time, hunters will once more begin their search for a bear.

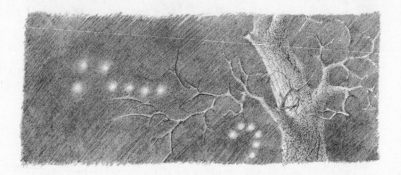

Signs

WHEN A HUNTER SEARCHES for a bear, he looks for big shuffling footmarks with monster toes; rocks overturned and stumps torn apart for insects; "scat," or bear droppings; limbs broken off fruit trees; scratches high on a tree trunk where a bear dug in to sharpen its claws; and other signs that may lead him to his prey.

In the Deer Yard

ON THE LAST DAY of the year in 1869, David Sturgis and Colvin Verplanck strapped on their snowshoes and went deer-hunting in upstate New York. But when they came upon the trail of a large bear, they decided to follow its tracks instead. They trailed that bear all that day, but they did not catch a glimpse of it.

The next morning, they continued the hunt. Sturgis and his hound Patsy followed the bear around one side of Burnt Mountain. Verplanck went in the opposite direction. He was searching for a place to wait in case the bear tried to go all the way around the mountain.

Soon he found a "deer yard," a place where deer came to feed. When he saw some old bear tracks nearby, he decided that was where he would wait.

"I seated myself on a stump," he said. "It was noon and the sun was bright and warm. Birds and squirrels chirped and frisked around. A quarter of an hour passed. Then miles away I faintly heard Patsy barking. Once, twice, three times I heard her, then no more.

"Half an hour passed, three-quarters of an hour. But there was nothing, and it grew tiresome. I felt I should get going, but once I had lost an elk by leaving too soon. So I waited.

"Another quarter of an hour passed. I was leaning forward with my rifle on my lap, getting drowsy, when I thought I heard a tramping sound far down the mountain. I sat up. Something was coming up the mountain in a long swinging canter."

Jump, jump. *JUMP, JUMP.* JUMP, JUMP, JUMP. *JUMP, JUMP, JUMP!*

"I heard it crashing through the bushes, go down into a hollow, come up out of the hollow. The creature was hidden by hemlock trees, but it sounded as if it was coming directly toward me.

"My rifle was at my shoulder and sighted. Another minute and it would clear the hemlocks. Suddenly it stopped. All was silent for one long minute. Then there was a slow questioning whine, then a snuffing and snorting—*so* wild, *so* peculiar.

"Then there was another whine, another series of snorts expressing doubt, surprise, anger. Aiming a little lower, I guessed its position behind the trees. Then I fired.

"With the explosion came a shrill scream of agony. No animal that I had shot before ever gave such a cry! It sounded human. Had I made a mistake? 'Oh! Oh! Oh!' I heard. 'Whew! Whew!'

"I heard it roll on the snow, then tumble into the hollow. I broke through the screen of hemlocks. About ten or fifteen feet down, a huge black bear was biting at the wound I had made in its side.

"When he saw me, he ran. I followed closely, firing once, twice, three times. Each time I fired, he turned and showed his teeth, as if the bullets had no effect. Then I fired once more. He leaped up on top of a cliff, started to run, then pitched forward and fell in a heap."

The Bear Hunt

BY ABRAHAM LINCOLN

"IF YOU HAVE NEVER seen a bear hunt, then you have lived in vain," wrote Abraham Lincoln. In this poem, he described a bear hunt of the kind he knew when he was growing up in southern Indiana in the 1820s.

Lincoln's language may seem stiff and old-fashioned, but chasing a bear was something he clearly enjoyed. He wrote this poem in the years after 1846 when he was becoming a national leader.

Of the twenty-two stanzas, the first sixteen are given here. In them, a bear picks up the scent of hunters and their dogs and tries to flee. The dogs bring him to bay, the hunters attack, and the bear fights back. Eventually, the bear is killed.

A wild bear chase didst never see?
Then hast thou lived in vain—
Thy richest bump of glorious glee
Lies desert in thy brain.

When first my father settled here,
'Twas then the frontier line;
The panther's screams filled night with fear
And bears preyed on the swine.

But woe for bruin's short-lived fun
When rose the squealing cry;
Now man and horse, with dog and gun
For vengeance at him fly.

A sound of danger strikes his ear;
He gives the breeze a snuff;
Away he bounds, with little fear,
And seeks the tangled rough.

On press his foes, and reach the ground
Where's left his half-munched meal;
The dogs, in circles, scent around
And find his fresh made trail.

With instant cry, away they dash,
And men as fast pursue;
O'er logs they leap, through water splash
And shout the brisk halloo.

Now to elude the eager pack
Bear shuns the open ground,
Through matted vines he shapes his track,
And runs it, round and round.

The tall, fleet cur, with deep-mouthed voice
Now speeds him, as the wind;
While half-grown pup, and short-legged mutt
Are yelping far behind.

And fresh recruits are dropping in
To join the merry corps;

With yelp and yell, a mingled din—
The woods are in a roar—

And round and round the chase now goes,
The world's alive with fun;
Nick Carter's horse his rider throws,
And Mose Hill drops his gun.

Now, sorely pressed, bear glances back,
And lolls his tired tongue,
When as, to force him from his track
An ambush on him sprung.

Across the glade he sweeps for flight,
And fully is in view—
The dogs, new fired by the sight
Their cry and speed renew.

The foremost ones now reach his rear;
He turns, they dash away,
And circling now the wrathful bear
They have him full at bay.

At top of speed the horsemen come,
All screaming in a row—
"Whoop!" "Take him, Tiger!" "Seize him, Drum!"
Bang—bang! the rifles go!

And furious now, the dogs he tears,
And crushes in his ire—
Wheels right and left, and upward rears,
With eyes of burning fire.

But leaden death is at his heart—
Vain all the strength he plies,
And, spouting blood from every part,
He reels, and sinks, and dies!

The Big Bear of Arkansas

ON A FINE FALL DAY, I was trailing for a b'ar when what should I see but fresh claw marks on the sassafras trees, about eight inches above any marks I knew of. Says I, "Them marks is a hoax, or it's the biggest b'ar that was ever grown."

The first time I hunted that critter, I saw him no less than three times, and each time he got away. My dogs chased him over eighteen miles and broke down, and my horse gave out, and I was as used up as a man can be.

Before I met that b'ar, such things were unknown to me. I caught every b'ar I set my mind to. But this one got so sassy that he helped himself to one of my hogs whenever he wanted one, and there was nothing I could do to stop him.

Missing that b'ar so often got to me. All I did was think about him. Finally, I made preparations to hunt him down once and for all. My friend Bill went with me. We started at sunrise. To my great joy, the dogs found his trail right off, and on and on we went. When we came to some open country, what should I see but that b'ar leisurely climbing a hill, and the dogs close at his heels. But he paid no attention.

On he went until he came to a tree. Its limbs formed a crotch about six feet from the ground, and he climbed up there and seated himself. The dogs were yelling all around him, but there he sat eyeing them as quiet as a pond.

My friend Bill reached shooting distance before me. He blazed away, hitting the critter in the center of the forehead. After the ball struck, the b'ar just shook his head. Then he got down from the tree as gently as a lady would get out of a carriage.

But he was in a rage. The way his eyes flashed—they would have singed a cat's hair. The dogs knew it and held back. Only one pup went near him, and the b'ar hit him so hard he entirely disappeared.

I turned to my fool friend, and I says, "Bill, you're a fool. You might as well tried to kill that b'ar by biting him. Now your shot has made a tiger of him."

Then I took aim at the b'ar's side, just back of his foreleg. I pulled the trigger—and my gun snapped! It was empty. I looked all over, but I couldn't find a cap anywhere. Now my wrath was really up. I had lost my caps. My gun had snapped. The fellow with me didn't know how to hunt. And because of him I expected that b'ar to kill a dozen of my dogs.

In that I was mistaken. The dogs had formed a ring around him, but the b'ar leaped over it. He gave a fierce growl and ran off again, with the dogs in full cry behind him.

Coming to the edge of a lake, the varmint jumped in and swam to a little island, which he reached just before the dogs did.

"I'll have him now," said I, for by then I had found my caps in the lining of my coat. Rolling a log into the lake, I paddled myself across to the island just as the dogs had cornered him in a thicket.

I rushed up and fired. At the same time, the critter leaped over the dogs. Running like mad, he jumped into the lake. He tried to mount the log I had just used, but every time he got on it, it rolled over and sent him under. Meanwhile, the dogs had jumped in and started pulling him about. Finally, my dog Bowie Knife clenched with him, and together they sunk into the lake.

Soon Bowie Knife came up alone, more dead than alive, and came ashore. But the b'ar stayed under. "Thank God," said I. "The old villain is dead at last."

I cut a grapevine for a rope and dove down to where I could see him in the water. I fastened the vine to his leg and fished him ashore.

But when I looked him over, it wasn't the old critter after all! It was a she-b'ar that I had fished ashore. The b'ar I was hunting had disappeared.

The way everything got mixed up on that island was very curious. Now I was convinced that I was hunting the devil himself. I went home that night and took to bed. But I was determined to catch that b'ar.

I rested my dogs. I took my rifle apart and oiled it. I put caps in every pocket I had. Then I told my neighbors that on Monday morning—I named the day—I would start that b'ar and bring him home with me.

Well, the day before I was supposed to go after him, I went into the woods near my house, taking my gun and my dog along just from habit. And what should I see going over my fence but that b'ar! The old varmint was within a hundred yards of me. He seemed so large, he loomed up like a black mist, and he walked right toward me.

I took deliberate aim, and fired. The varmint wheeled around, gave a yell, and fell through the fence like a tree falling through a cobweb. By the time I reached him, he was dead.

I never liked the way I hunted him time and again and missed. There is something curious about that I could never understand. And I never was satisfied at his giving in so easy in the end. Perhaps he had heard of my preparations to hunt him the next day, so he just came in to save us both the trouble. But that isn't likely. My private opinion is that he was an unhuntable b'ar, that he died only when his time come.

"Grandfather,
Please Forgive Us..."

INDIANS WORSHIPPED BEARS. They were one of the sacred animals in their religion. They believed that bears were their ancient ancestors and relatives, that once upon a time Indians who died came back to life as bears. When they spoke of a bear, they called it "Grandfather," or "Cousin," or "Elder Brother."

As a result, some tribes would not kill a bear or eat its meat. It would be like killing and eating a member of their family, they believed. Others would hunt a bear, but only if they needed the food badly, and that was a different kind of hunt from any other.

Often it was in the winter, when food was scarce and the bears were in their dens. Before the hunters started out, they prayed that they would find a bear and kill it. In some tribes, a bear dance was part of this ritual. Members of the tribe dressed in bearskins, or they wore masks made from the heads of bears. They shuffled and swayed and clawed the air the way bears do, and they asked the Bear Spirit to be kind to them.

When the hunters found a den, they stood outside and called to the bear. They might call, "Grandfather, please come out. Our children are hungry, and we need food." Then, with spears and arrows, they roused the bear and killed it. Then they apologized for having done so. "Grandfather, please forgive us," they would say.

If it was possible, they carried the bear's body back to camp. There members of the tribe honored it and mourned its death.

In some tribes, they cleaned the bear's coat and decorated it with beads and bits of colored cloth. They might give it a headdress to wear. Then they seated it in a place of honor and sang songs of mourning to it.

The men who had hunted the bear came before it. They praised its courage and thanked it for the food. The hunter who actually killed the bear smoked a pipe of peace with it. He smoked first. Then he blew the smoke into the bear's mouth so that the bear could take part.

The bear was then skinned, and the meat was cooked and eaten. The hunter who had killed the bear was given a piece of the bear's heart to eat. This was to give him courage for the future.

Often the entire tribe would feast upon the meat, but nothing was wasted. Every part of the bear was used, except the bones. These were buried in the ground or placed on a burial platform in the same position they had when the bear was alive. In this way the bear could come to life again.

If it was all done properly, the hunters would find another bear when the tribe was in need of food again. The Bear Spirit would see to that.

These are old beliefs and practices, but some of them are still followed, for the bear is still thought of as a special animal.

REWARD

DEAD OR ALIVE

OUTLAW BEARS

When food was scarce, hungry bears raided ranches and farms. They smashed fences, broke into buildings, killed and ate the livestock, and stole other food. Ranchers and farmers called them "outlaw bears." There were all sorts of schemes to kill them. But some bears went on with their raids for years before they were caught, and others never were caught.

Of course, many stories grew up about these bears. People even gave them names by which they became known in their territories. There were "Old Mose," "Old Ephraim," "Old Brin," "Clubfoot," and hundreds of others. You will meet some of them in this chapter.

Old Mose

"OLD MOSE" WAS A GIANT GRIZZLY that lived in the mountains of Colorado before the turn of the century. To the ranchers nearby, he was a plague. Over the years, he had killed and eaten over eight hundred of their cattle, along with dozens of horses, sheep, and hogs. The cattle alone would be worth at least half a million dollars today.

Usually there was a reward out for Old Mose, and usually there were hunters and trappers on the lookout for him. He was easy to identify from the tracks he left behind. Two toes were missing from his left hind foot. But he was not easy to catch. Over the years, he killed at least five hunters who had managed to corner him.

It was said that Old Mose never attacked a human unless that person threatened him. Yet he seemed to enjoy scaring people half to death. He was known for sneaking up on campsites, rushing in with a loud roar, and stampeding men and horses in all directions. Then he would go on his way.

He was finally killed in 1904. A pack of hunting dogs

brought him to bay, and a hunter shot him eight times. Old Mose was at least forty years old when he died, a remarkable age for a wild bear. His teeth were still sound, and he appeared to have been in excellent health. Had he not been killed, he might have continued his raids and pranks for several years more.

The Bear Trap

THERE WAS ANOTHER GRIZZLY in Colorado that had been raiding cattle ranches. If this one had a name, it has not come down to us. No matter what scheme the ranchers tried, they could not stop him. As a last resort, they offered a thousand-dollar reward to anyone who killed the bear.

There was a trapper who decided that he could do it. He had it all worked out. He got hold of an old cow, and he took her down to the end of a ravine and tied her to a tree. She was the bait to attract the bear.

Next he set up three spring guns around her. The guns guarded all the approaches. Each had a silk line attached to the trigger, and each line was stretched over the bushes or tall grass that grew there. If the bear moved one of the lines, the gun to which it was attached would fire at him. That was the outer defense.

Then the trapper hid three forty-pound traps around the cow. If the bear managed to get by the spring guns, one of the traps would get him. That was the inner defense. It all looked something like this:

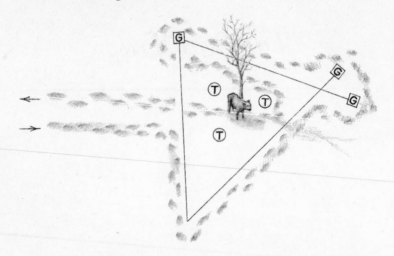

The first night after everything was ready, it snowed and the bear did not appear. But the next night, he paid the cow a visit. The tracks he left in the snow told the story.

When the bear picked up the cow's scent, or first heard her, he was more than a mile away. He came right down the ravine toward her. But when he found one of the silk lines, he stopped. He walked all the way around the outer defense, looking for an opening. When he could not find one, he jumped over one of the lines.

He then walked around the cow several times—and found the traps. He squeezed between two of them and killed the cow. After feeding on her, he dragged the carcass across the two unused traps, which sprang them. Then he jumped back over the silk line and left.

The next morning the trapper reset the two traps the bear had sprung. He also added a trap at the place where the bear had jumped over the silk line. Then he set up a spring gun along the trail the bear had taken down the ravine.

That night the bear returned. Again his tracks in the snow told the story. When he came down the ravine, he found the line to the new spring gun. He walked around it, then continued on his way.

When he got to the outer defense, he also found the new trap and jumped over the line at another place. He avoided the traps around the cow's carcass, had a good meal, and went on his way.

The next morning, the trapper decided to try once more. He built a pen of logs around what was left of the carcass, using a big rock as the back of the pen. Then he set two more traps, one at the entrance to the pen and one inside.

Now the giant trap he had built looked like this:

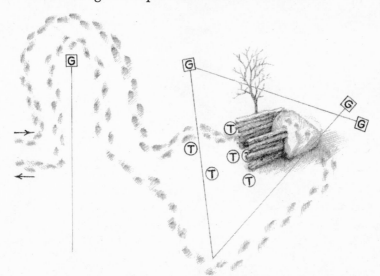

When the bear returned that night, he jumped over one of the silk lines. Then he climbed up on the big rock. From there he reached down and dragged up the carcass. In doing so, he knocked over some of the logs that made up the pen. The logs fell across a line attached to a spring gun, and the gun went off.

The bear climbed down from the rock and examined the gun. Then he went back to his meal. When there was nothing more to eat, he stepped over the line where the logs rested on it and went back down the canyon.

Frank Clark Kills Old Ephraim

OLD EPHRAIM WAS A GIANT GRIZZLY BEAR that raided sheep ranches in northern Utah. Frank Clark was a forest ranger and sheepherder who managed to trap and kill this bear after ten years of trying. This is how he recalled that night.

"Ephraim had a large pool he had scooped out of a spring in a little canyon. At least once a week he would come to wallow in it. I used to set my trap in there, but every time he visited the pool, he would pick up the trap and set it off to one side.

"When Ephraim dug a new pool just below the old one, I set my trap in there and stirred up the mud to cover it. The trap was attached with a chain to a fifteen-foot log. He would have to trail that log behind him if he got caught and tried to escape.

"My camp was about a mile downstream from the trap. It was a beautiful cool night, and after supper I lighted my pipe and set my gaze at the stars. My nearest company was some other sheepherders about four miles away and my horses in a meadow below my camp.

"After bedding down for the night and sleeping for some time, I was suddenly awakened by the most unearthly sounds I have ever heard. Usually my dog would bark at anything out of the ordinary, but this time he did not. After the first cry, there was a grumbling sound. Then there was a roar that echoed from canyon wall to canyon wall. It was clear that I had trapped a bear—if not Ephraim, then another one.

"I quickly slipped on my shoes, grabbed my rifle, and started down the trail. From the sounds the bear was making, he was at the bottom of the canyon and coming closer. Soon the noise was in the willows along the creek bed just below me.

"After the bear passed, I slipped down to a trail along the creek. In the bright moonlight, I could see his tracks. I followed the noise down the creek until I reached a point near my camp. There, crashing out of the creek bottom, came Ephraim on his hind legs. On his left foreleg he carried my trap, which weighed twenty-seven pounds. Around his right foreleg he had wrapped fifteen feet of log chain.

"As he came toward me, I was chilled to the bone with fear. I stood watching as he approached. I did not try to shoot. Finally, out of fear more than anything, I opened up with my small .25/35 caliber rifle and pumped six shots into him. He fell dead at my feet. I suddenly became sorry that I had killed this giant bear."

Frank Clark later found that Old Ephraim had broken the big log attached to the trap into several pieces. The bear then walked over a mile on his hind legs while holding the trap and the chain in front of him. He was buried near the ranger's campsite in the Cache National Forest in Utah. His grave marker reads:

OLD EPHRAIM'S
GRAVE

KILLED BY
FRANK CLARK
MALAD IDAHO

AUGUST 22, 1923
WEIGHT APPROX. 1100 POUNDS
HEIGHT 9 FEET 11 INCHES

SMITHSONIAN INSTITUTE
HAS EPHRAIM'S SKULL

Star Breast

BECAUSE HE HAD A WHITE MARK on his front, the bear was called Star Breast. He lived in the mountains in northern Mexico near a spring where two trails crossed. Once it had been a popular place for travelers to stop. But because of Star Breast, not many people stopped there any more.

He would lie in wait for them. Then he would attack them and eat them if he could. Very few bears behave that way. But Star Breast was an unusual bear. He was larger than most bears, and smarter, and bullets did not seem to harm him.

One day two *vaqueros*, or cowboys, rode into that part of the mountains looking for horses that had strayed. But what they found was fresh bear tracks—tracks so large that they could have belonged only to Star Breast.

These cowboys knew about him. One of them, named Pablo Romero, said, "If I see that bear, I will kill him. It is useless to shoot at him, and we have no guns anyhow. But I have a new *reata* [lariat] that would hold an elephant. And

I have my roping horse. He has the strength of ten bulls in him. I will rope that bear and choke him to death."

The other cowboy was against it. "Right now he is hiding in those bushes down there listening to us and preparing to come after us," he said. "Instead of riding toward him, let's get out of here."

But Pablo would not change his mind, and they continued on. As they moved down the trail, Star Breast burst out of the bushes. He stood on his hind legs, waving his great hairy arms, then rumbled a great roar and came toward them.

Pablo's friend retreated, then stopped and watched. Pablo untied his lariat and fastened one end to the saddle horn. From the other end, he played out a loop of rope. Swinging the rope back and forth, he rode toward Star Breast.

As he dashed by, Pablo hurled the loop toward him. As he had planned, it fell over Star Breast's head. But it also caught him under one of his arms, something that Pablo had not planned for.

When his horse suddenly reached the end of the lariat, they were moving so fast that the rope jerked the horse back and pulled the bear down. As Star Breast got to his feet, the horse quickly whirled around to get a better pull the next time.

Now came a desperate contest between a fierce, powerful, cunning bear at one end of the rope and a trained horse and an expert rider at the other end. Several times Star Breast was jerked down, but each time he scrambled to his feet. Had the rope caught him only around the neck, it would have choked him by now.

But Star Breast soon learned that he could break the force of the rope by grasping it with his paws. Then he began to go forward up the rope toward the horse. The more rope he took, the closer to the horse he got. The closer he got, the less room there was for the horse to run. With less room to run, he could no longer pull the bear to the ground or jerk the rope out of his paws.

As Star Breast got closer and closer, Pablo realized that they could no longer stop the bear. Soon he would be close enough to attack them.

Pablo Romero was a brave man. He would not run off and leave his horse to a bear. Yet he had no gun to shoot. And with the rope knotted so tightly about the saddle horn, he could not loosen it. Still worse, on this day he had no knife with which to cut it. Had the other cowboy been brave enough, he might have roped the bear and pulled him away. He was not that brave.

Panting and frothing, Star Breast at last reached the horse and the man. Now the other cowboy saw a strange thing. He saw Star Breast reach up and drag Pablo Romero from the saddle and throw him to the ground. He saw him take the rope from his neck, coil it up, and tie it to the saddle horn. Then he saw him throw Pablo's limp body across the horse, climb into the saddle, and ride off into the brush. That was the last anyone ever saw of Pablo Romero or his horse.

GRIZZLY, LADY, AND BEN

There are many stories of people who obtain a bear cub and try to raise it as a pet. Usually these stories do not have a happy ending, for most bears cannot live by human rules.

Eventually the bear is returned to the woods or is given to a zoo or is destroyed. Or it dies at the hands of a hunter who does not realize that it is tame.

Only once in a great while does someone succeed in raising a bear and sharing its life. Perhaps the best-known example is that of James Capen Adams. In the 1840s Adams worked in Massachusetts, first as a shoemaker, then for a small carnival as a collector of wild animals.

In 1849, with thousands of others, he journeyed to California in search of gold. In 1852, when he was forty-five years old, he took to the mountains as a hunter and trapper. He built a cabin in the Sierra Nevada 160 miles east of San Francisco and earned his living selling animals he captured and animal skins.

He probably would be forgotten by now if it were not for Lady Washington, Ben Franklin, and other grizzly bears he tamed and made his companions and helpers. Because of them he is remembered as "Grizzly" Adams.

GRIZZLY CAPTURES
LADY WASHINGTON

IN THE SPRING OF 1853, Grizzly Adams set out from his camp in the Sierra Nevada on his first hunting and trapping expedition. His plan was to capture a number of bears, panthers, wolves, and other wild animals and send them by ship to Boston, where his brother would sell them.

With him were two Sierra Indians, Stanislaus and Tuolumne, who were his assistants. There also was a hunter from Texas named Sykesey. They made their way across Oregon to the eastern part of the Washington Territory, or what is now Montana.

Soon after they set up a base camp, they killed a female grizzly bear and managed to lasso two of her cubs. Grizzly decided to raise one of them for his own. He called her Lady Washington. "She was the prettiest little animal in all the country," he said.

But Lady was also more than a year old and was wild and short-tempered and missed her freedom. At first, Grizzly kept her chained to a tree. He tried to tame her with kindness, but whenever he went near her, she lunged and snapped at him. When finally she clawed him, he took steps to improve her behavior.

"I cut a stout stick and with it began to warm her jacket," he said. "It made her furious. It is hard to describe her violence, her snarls, her frothing anger. Not that she was hurt, but she had worked herself into a frenzy." But Grizzly kept at it until, in her anger, Lady wore herself out. Only then did she allow him to pat her coat and feed her.

Beating her that way troubled Grizzly. "It was a cruel spectacle to see a man whip a chained animal," he said later. But Lady was getting to be a big, dangerous bear. Already she was set in her ways. If he was going to tame her, he explained, he had no choice.

Each time she lost her temper after that, he rapped her a few times with a stick. Soon he was able to lead her on a chain. Then she followed him without being led. After a while, she ate with him, slept where he slept, and went along on hunting trips. By then Lady probably weighed three hundred pounds, but she behaved like a big, affectionate dog.

GRIZZLY AND LADY
MEET A BEAR

Grizzly, Sykesey, and the two Indians had spent the day in the woods building a bear trap out of logs. Lady Washington was with them. Toward evening, they started back to camp.

Grizzly asked the others to kill any game they could find on the way. He gave them his rifle. Then he and Lady headed back. They had not gone far when suddenly she snorted, then chattered her teeth.

"At this I wheeled around," Grizzly said. "Right behind her, in full sight, standing on its hind legs, stood a savage old bear. There I was without a real weapon and with Lady as well as myself to protect.

"I seized her chain, which was wrapped around her neck, and unwound it as quietly as possible. Meanwhile, the enemy dropped to all fours and came closer. Then he rose up again. I knew that if I moved, he would instantly attack or instantly flee. I stood stock still with my pistol in my hand.

"Suddenly I fired the pistol in the air. Then I rattled Lady's chain and started yelling as loud as I could. At the same time, Lady began to growl. Frightened out of his wits, the bear turned tail and ran. I followed after him yelling and shouting and clanking the chain. It must have seemed to that bear that a thousand devils had sprung up all at once, and they were all after him."

LADY, THE PACK BEAR

GRIZZLY SOON TRIED TO TRAIN Lady to carry a pack. He started with an old flour sack he had filled with sand. He tied it tightly across her back. But it was hardly in place before she tore a hole in it with her teeth and the sand ran out.

"I talked to her," Grizzly said. "I tried to make her understand, but it was no use. She just got angry."

On another day, about four or five miles from camp, Grizzly killed a fat buck. It was too heavy for him to carry by himself. So he split it into two parts and lashed half of it to Lady's back. She tried first to tear it off with her teeth. When that did not work, she rolled over on her back and tried to get it off that way. Both times he shouted at her and rapped her with a stick. Then she gave in and carried the load home.

After that she regularly carried provisions, equipment,

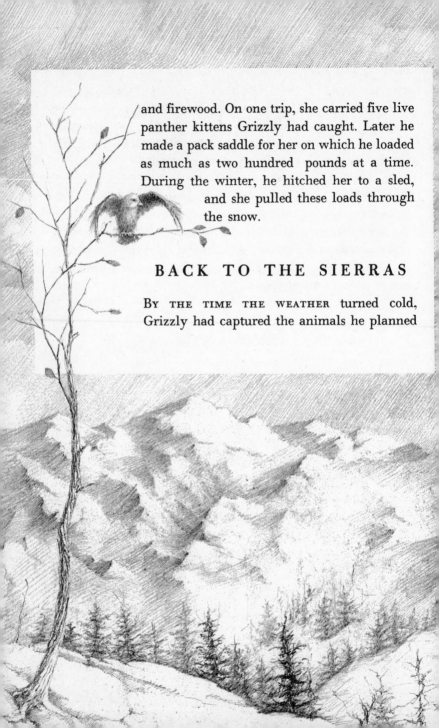

and firewood. On one trip, she carried five live panther kittens Grizzly had caught. Later he made a pack saddle for her on which he loaded as much as two hundred pounds at a time. During the winter, he hitched her to a sled, and she pulled these loads through the snow.

BACK TO THE SIERRAS

By the time the weather turned cold, Grizzly had captured the animals he planned to send to his brother in Boston. The next step was to move them to Portland, Oregon, then have them loaded on a ship.

It was more than three hundred miles to Portland along old Indian trails through mountains and deep woods. To make the trip, Grizzly organized a packtrain. He hired six more Indians and two more white hunters as helpers. He also rented thirty horses and mules from their tribe. They carried animal skins, food, and boxes containing live wolves, foxes, fishers, and bear cubs. Grizzly drove the larger animals along on foot. There were six bears, four wolves, four deer, four antelope, and two elks in his herd.

After more than a month in the wilderness, they arrived in Portland. The animals and the food they needed for the

rest of the journey were loaded aboard the bark *Mary Ann* for the trip around Cape Horn to Boston. The Texan Sykesey decided to stay in Oregon for a while. With Tuolumne, Stanislaus, and Lady Washington, Grizzly headed back to his camp in the Sierra Nevada. There they spent the winter and the first months of 1854.

CAUGHT IN A SNOWSTORM

DURING A HUNTING TRIP that winter, Grizzly, Stanislaus, and Lady were caught in a snowstorm and forced to spend the night under a pine tree. The two men built a rousing fire, but, in the severe cold, Stanislaus became ill and needed all the blankets they had with them. To keep himself from freezing, Grizzly decided to sleep next to Lady.

"I coaxed her as near the fire as possible," he said. "Then I lay down with her shaggy coat on one side of me and the fire on the other side. Once during the night, she arose and left, but soon she came back, lapped my hands for a moment, and nestled down again. It was late in the morning before I awakened. My shaggy companion was still sleeping peacefully."

GRIZZLY CAPTURES
BEN FRANKLIN

WHEN SPRING RETURNED, Grizzly went hunting in the Yosemite Valley, about forty miles southeast of his camp. Tuolumne and a hunter named Solon went with him. So did the bear Lady, a greyhound dog he had captured and tamed, and her new pups.

There, in the Mariposa Canyon, Grizzly found the den of a huge she-bear. From the sounds he heard inside, he knew that she had newborn cubs with her. He decided to kill the bear and take her cubs, as he had done when he captured Lady Washington.

For three days and nights, he hid in a thicket in front of the den, waiting for the bear to appear. When his patience ran out, he fired his rifle into the air, hoping that the sound would attract her. When it didn't, he crawled up to the mouth of the den and shouted into it.

"A moment later," Grizzly said, "there was a booming sound in the den, like the sound of a train engine in a tunnel. Then the enraged animal rushed out, growling and snapping. She rose up on her hind legs, and I fired at her."

After Grizzly had killed the bear, he crawled into her den. "I kneeled and tried to peer inside," he said, "but all was dark and silent. What dangers might lurk in that gloom, it was impossible to tell.

"I carefully loaded my rifle and my pistol. I took a small torch of pine splinters from my pocket and lighted it. I left my rifle at the mouth of the den. With the torch in my left hand and the pistol in my right hand, I crawled in.

"The entrance was a rough hole that extended inward for about six feet. There I found a small room six to eight feet across and about five feet high. The entire floor was carpeted with leaves and grass.

"As I crawled around, I heard a rustling sound in the leaves. Bending down with my torch, I found two little cubs. They could not have been over a week old, for their eyes were still closed. I placed them in my bosom, between my buckskin and my woolen shirt, and I crawled out."

Grizzly gave one of the cubs to his friend Solon and kept the other for himself. He named his cub Ben Franklin. Since they needed milk, Grizzly fed the cubs a mixture of flour, sugar, and water. It was the closest he could come to milk, but it was not the answer.

Then he remembered that the greyhound had milk. She was still nursing her new pups. Grizzly destroyed two of the pups, then gave the dog the two bear cubs to feed in their place. At first she snapped at the cubs and bit them. But after a while she let them feed side by side with her only remaining pup. To keep the cubs from scratching her with their claws, Grizzly made four pairs of buckskin mittens, which he put on them each time they were fed.

After four or five weeks, Grizzly got them to eat some meat he had pounded with a rock and made tender, and they no longer had to depend on the dog's milk.

Ben Franklin was far easier to train than Lady Washington. Unlike Lady, he had lived only a few days as a wild bear, not a year, as she had, and he did not have to learn new ways of behaving. At times he seemed more like a dog than a bear. In fact, a dog was his constant companion. It was Rambler, the greyhound pup who was raised with him.

AN EXPEDITION
TO THE ROCKY MOUNTAINS

In April, Grizzly and the two Indians headed east toward the Rocky Mountains on another hunting expedition. They would be gone a year and travel more than two thousand miles. They traveled in an old wagon drawn by a pair of oxen and a pair of mules. Lady, Ben Franklin, and Rambler all went along. Lady was fastened to the rear axle with a long chain. Ben and Rambler, both still very young, rode in the wagon or ran alongside.

Their journey took them east through the Sierra Nevada and the Humboldt Range, then across two hundred miles of desert to the Rockies. It was a difficult journey. As they moved through the desert, men and animals alike suffered from thirst and exhaustion. They rationed their water, but often they could not find enough to refill their water bags. For a time, the animals had so little strength, they could only stagger along.

Ben Franklin's feet were also a problem. They became so sore from walking on sharp rocks and hot sand that Grizzly feared they would be badly injured. He tried to keep Ben in the wagon until they healed, but the bear would not stay put. So Grizzly made Ben two pairs of moccasins from animal hides. He tied them on so tightly that the cub could not remove them. When Grizzly took them off two weeks later, Ben's feet had healed.

As they traveled east, they hunted everywhere they could. When they reached Salt Lake City on July 3, after almost three months of traveling, they had hides, bear meat, and young wild animals to sell. Then they headed farther east into the mountains and set up a hunting camp where they sold meat to settlers moving west.

LADY WASHINGTON'S
ROMANCE

LATE ONE NIGHT, a male grizzly bear stole into camp and spent an hour making Lady Washington's acquaintance. Then he peacefully left. One of Grizzly's helpers wanted to kill him, but Grizzly would not allow it.

The next two nights, the bear came back to see her again. Then he returned to the woods. The following year, 1855, she gave birth to the visitor's cub. Grizzly named it Frémont for John Charles Frémont, the explorer who helped to open the western United States to settlement.

BEN AND RAMBLER
SAVE GRIZZLY'S LIFE

WHEN THEY RETURNED from the Rockies in 1855, Grizzly spent a few days at his cabin in the Sierras relaxing.

Heading back to camp one day with Ben and Rambler, he heard a stick crack. He turned in time to see a huge grizzly, with three cubs at her side, about to spring at him.

"I tried to raise my rifle," he said, "but the bear struck it from my hand. With the same blow, she knocked me to the ground. Both Ben and Rambler rushed forward to attack her. Rambler seized the enemy's thigh. Ben attacked her at the throat. Meanwhile, I snatched my rifle and sprang to one side.

"When the bear attacked Ben, biting his head and neck, I gave a terrific shout. When she rose up again on her hind legs, I shot her, and she fell over on her back. When I looked for Ben, he was bounding off toward camp, with blood streaming from his head and sides, yelling at every leap.

"At first I did not know that I was hurt. But in a little while I realized that my scalp had been badly torn, and that I had been bitten in many places. I managed to reach camp only with the greatest difficulty. I found Ben under the wagon licking his sides. I took him into the cabin and dressed his wounds before I dressed my own."

A PARADE IN NEW YORK

IN 1856 GRIZZLY GAVE UP his life in the woods. The many injuries he had received in his fights with bears and other animals had weakened his health. He settled in San Francisco with Lady, Ben Franklin, Rambler, and his other animals. They moved into a dark, dingy basement at 142 Clay Street, where Grizzly ran the Mountaineer Museum. The bears were on chains fastened to bolts in the floor. The other animals were in cages. For twenty-five cents, a visitor could see them all, then watch Grizzly wrestle with the bears and ride on a bear's back.

Almost every day, Grizzly and his big bears walked through the city with a crowd of children and yelping dogs at their heels. With his long white beard and his fringed buckskins, and all the bears around him, he was a splendid sight.

In that period, Grizzly dictated the story of his adventures to Theodore H. Hittell, a newspaper reporter who turned them into a book, *The Adventures of James Capen Adams: Mountaineer and Grizzly Bear Hunter of California*. The adventures in this chapter are based on that book.

A few months later, Grizzly moved the museum to a larger building at Clay and Kearny streets, and changed its name to the Pacific Museum. He added monkeys, snakes, and sea lions, and a band that played every night.

In 1858 Ben Franklin became ill and died. Two years later, Grizzly closed the museum and left California. He put his animals aboard the clipper ship *Golden Fleece* and sailed with them around Cape Horn to New York.

Soon after Grizzly arrived, he sold a half-interest in his animal show to the famous showman P. T. Barnum. His animals then performed for several weeks at Barnum's American Museum. The day the show opened, there was a big parade down Broadway with a brass band, and Grizzly and his bears led the way.

CHARLTON, MASSACHUSETTS

No one who saw Grizzly perform could have known that he was in great pain and was dying. Five years earlier, a grizzly he had shot had all but torn off his scalp. Since then, other bears had reopened the wound. In New York, a doctor told him that his head was beyond repair, that he had only a short time to live.

Grizzly sold Barnum the remaining half-interest in his animal show, and Barnum hired a new trainer to take over when he left. When his strength finally ran out, Grizzly went home to Massachusetts to die.

He was buried in the town of Charlton, west of Boston. Carved on his gravestone are a hunter and a bear, and an inscription that begins: "And silent now the hunter lays . . ."

CAPTIVES

O ver the years, many bears have been taken captive. Some were full-grown bears that were used to fight ferocious dogs or wild bulls while hundreds of people watched. But most were bear cubs that were stolen from their mother's den or captured after she had been killed.

They were raised and trained to carry out all sorts of tasks. It is said that some carried loads on their backs, turned grinding wheels in mills, and pulled wagons, sleds, and plows. Others danced and performed tricks on street corners or in carnivals.

In modern times, any bears needed come from animal dealers and zoos. They appear in circuses and movies and on TV. They have also been used in scientific experiments. In one case, bears in a military plane flew at twice the speed of sound, then traveled back to earth in an aluminum capsule. What happened on those flights is described later in this chapter.

Fighting Bears

SACKERSON AND OLD NELL

THERE WAS A TIME in England when bears fought packs of dogs. For hundreds of years, people flocked to see these fights at outdoor arenas called "bear gardens." What they saw was a bear chained to a stake fighting for its life against four or five vicious bulldogs or mastiffs.

If a bear killed or injured one of these dogs, another was quickly sent in to replace it. Often spectators brought their own dogs to try against a bear. The fight continued until the supply of dogs ran out or the bear was killed or was too badly injured to go on.

This was called "bearbaiting." There were "baits" for over seven hundred years in England until 1835, when Parliament finally banned them for their cruelty. In that period, bearbaiting was as popular in England as soccer is today.

Yet there were no wild bears in England in those days. There had not been any since the eleventh century. Some of the bears needed for the baits may have been raised on bear farms. But most were brought in from other countries.

Some bears fought in cities and towns all over England. They were as well known as modern athletes are and had fans who rooted for them and came to see them fight. The biggest stars included Tom of Lincoln, Ned of Canterbury, Don Jon, George Stone, Old Nell of Middlewich, and Sackerson.

Sackerson was probably the most famous fighting bear. He was even mentioned in a play by William Shakespeare, *The Merry Wives of Windsor*. One of the characters boasts that he has seen Sackerson running loose in the streets twenty times, and each time, as women cried and shrieked, he recaptured him.

For many years there was a "Master of Bears" in England, who was appointed by the King or Queen. He was in charge of all bearbaiting, just as today in the United States the commissioner of baseball oversees that sport.

A fighting bear was usually owned by a town or a business or some other group. A good fighting bear could earn quite a bit of money for its owners. Usually it was tended by a keeper called a "bearward." He was something like the manager of a prizefighter. His job was to arrange for his bear to fight at baits, care for it at these fights, and nurse it back to health when it was injured.

Some bearwards had close relationships with their bears. After a bait, Old Nell used to share a glass of ale with her bearward at the Red Cow Inn in Middlewich, or so it was said.

GENERAL SCOTT

IN 1853 A POSTER on a tree in Placerville, California, announced a fight between a bull and a bear:

War!   War!!   War!!!
The celebrated bull-killing bear
GENERAL SCOTT
will fight a bull on Sunday, the 15th inst.
at 2 p.m. on Moquelumne Hill.
The Bear will be chained with a 20-foot
chain in the middle of the arena. The bull
will be perfectly wild, young, of Spanish
breed and the best that can be found in
the country.

On that day, the wooden stands were jammed with people who had paid five dollars to get in. Until the fight began, two fiddlers played popular tunes. General Scott, the bear, waited in the middle of the arena locked in a heavy wooden cage with iron bars. One of his legs was fastened to a stake by a long chain. Two bulls waited in pens at the other end. If the bull that fought the bear was injured, the other one would be sent in to help him.

There was a great deal of excitement that day. In previous fights, General Scott had beaten several bulls, but the bulls had not been treated fairly. The sharp tips of their horns had been sawed off. They had also been tied to the bear by a long rope. In this fight, the bull would run free, and his horns would not be tampered with.

The bear was introduced to the crowd, and his cage was opened. Then one of the bulls was let out of his pen. The bear crouched and waited. The bull stood quietly for several seconds, then lowered his head and charged furiously across the arena.

He crashed into the bear's side with a loud thud, knocking him to the ground. Then the bear rolled over on his back and grabbed the bull's nose between his teeth, and his neck with his forepaws. The bull stamped on the bear with his hind legs. The bear shook the bull so savagely by the nose that he threw him to the ground. The bull quickly got to his feet and broke away. Then he charged at the bear again. But the bear again grabbed him by the nose, then by a hind leg. He so badly injured the bull that the animal lay down to regain its strength.

The second bull was sent in to help. He charged across the arena at full tilt, but the bear quickly grabbed him by the nose. Struggling violently, he knocked the bear over. Then the other bull joined the attack.

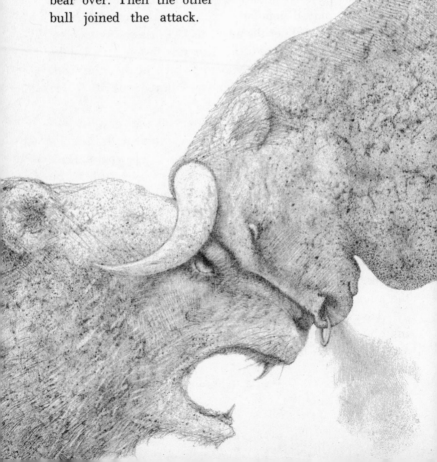

But it soon was clear that even together the two bulls were no match for the General. He was declared the winner, and the bulls were shot and put out of their pain. A few weeks later it was General Scott who went down to defeat. A bull killed him with his first charge.

BEAR FIGHTING

CONTESTS BETWEEN BEARS and bulls in America went back to the eighteenth century, when Mexico owned California. Mexicans began to settle there and brought this tradition with them. The fights did not die out until the 1870s, more than twenty years after California became one of the United States. In Southern California, where the largest number of Mexicans lived, these fights were held to help celebrate religious feast days and other holidays. To the north, in towns like Placerville and cities like San Francisco, promoters put on the fights only to make money.

The bulls and the grizzly bears that were needed were plentiful in California. They could be captured outside many towns. The bulls were found in roving herds of wild cattle and taken with lassos.

To catch a grizzly was more complicated. Some hunters used a trap that looked like a log cabin without a floor. They suspended it between two trees and hung a piece of raw meat inside. When a bear grabbed the meat, the trap came down.

In the Mexican parts of California, often a grizzly was caught with lassos, then hog-tied. Usually four men were needed to capture a bear that way. The most highly skilled were called *lazadores*, or ropers. Usually these were ranchers who were expert horsemen and experts at handling a lasso.

To them, roping a grizzly was the greatest of sports. When a bear was needed for a feast day, they dressed themselves and their horses in beautiful costumes, then rode off to find one.

When they spied a bear they wanted, they drove it into the open, then surrounded it. The idea was to catch one of the bear's forelegs with a rope. Another *lazador* then had to quickly catch a second leg. But even with two ropes in place and two horses pulling in opposite directions, a thousand-pound bear could break away and easily kill a horse and its rider. Only when the bear was on its back, only when all four ropes were in place with a horse pulling each—only then would the *lazadores* send up a cheer.

Yet the most dangerous part was still to come. At that point a *lazador* dismounted, leaving it to his horse to keep the rope taut. Carrying another lasso, he moved as close as he dared to the bear. Then he slipped a noose around the bear's forelegs and pulled the rope tight. Now a second *lazador* dismounted. With another lasso, the two tied up the bear's hind legs and bound his jaws together. Only then was the bear hauled off to fight the bull.

Performing Bears

MARTIN

THERE WAS A TIME in Europe and America when bears danced on street corners. When a crowd had collected, the bear leader jerked sharply on a chain around the bear's neck, and the bear rose up on its hind legs.

Then the bear leader would beat a tambourine. In Romany, the gypsy language, he would call, *"Adje malo, Martine, da poigras, de de!"*—"Dance a little, Martin, come on, come on!" Many dancing bears were named Martin. When the bear heard the tambourine, it would move its feet more or less in time to the music.

After it danced, it might perform other tricks the bear leader had taught it. It might wrestle with the leader, ride a hobbyhorse, lie on its stomach and snore, or climb a tall pole. After each trick, the leader would give the bear a lump of sugar or a piece of candy to reward it and keep it calm.

At the end of the performance, the leader or his wife or their children walked through the crowd holding out a cup for contributions. "For the bear," they would say. Sometimes

the bear itself went around with the cup.
The leader, his family, and the bear all
lived on what they collected.

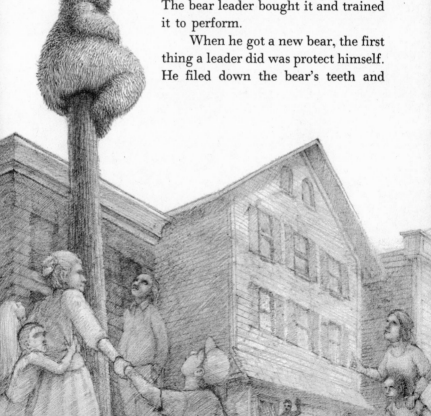

Before the First World War, danc-
ing bears and their leaders were a common sight. The bear
leader was usually a gypsy from Bulgaria, Romania, or one
of the other countries in southeastern Europe. The bear was
usually a Eurasian brown bear from the Carpathian Mountains in that region.

Most often the bear had been
stolen from its mother's den when it
was a cub and carried off in a sack.
The bear leader bought it and trained
it to perform.

When he got a new bear, the first
thing a leader did was protect himself.
He filed down the bear's teeth and

claws. He fastened a muzzle around its mouth. He put a collar around its neck and a ring through its nose. Then he attached a chain to the collar and, in some cases, another chain to the nose ring.

To train the bear to "dance," he used a red-hot slab of stone. The bear was led out onto the hot surface on all fours, then jerked back into a sitting position. When the stone burned its bottom, the bear reared up on its hind legs. When its feet started to burn, it quickly lifted one foot, then the other, to ease the pain. As it did so, someone beat a tambourine and sang the songs to which it would later dance.

Over and over, day after day, the bear was led onto the red-hot stone. After a while, the music alone was enough to remind the bear of the pain. When the music started, the bear would move quickly from foot to foot—and "dance."

TRAINING BEARS TODAY

FEW BEARS DANCE on street corners any more, but bears still perform. There are circus bears that drive motorcycles, ride bicycles, balance on big plastic balls, pull wagons, and even roller skate. And there are others that appear on television or in movies.

These bears are said to be treated more humanely than in the past. Before they are trained, they are likely to have their claws removed to protect against injury. But in earlier times they also may have had their teeth pulled out or filed down, as we have seen, or they may have had their paws broken, so that they could not use them as weapons. If they were males, they may have been castrated, to make them easier to handle.

The training itself seems to be more humane. Most trainers today are said to use a system of rewards to train their animals. The steps in a trick are repeated again and again until they become a part of the animal. If the animal does something right, it is rewarded. Usually it is given a treat of food and some praise.

But when it does not obey or succeed, there is no treat, and there may be a scolding. This approach requires great patience and is costly, for it may take several months, even a year or two, to train an animal properly.

In years past, critics, including trainers, have objected to the use of whips, electric prods, sharp hooks, and other cruel methods of training which break an animal's spirit but teach it to perform quickly and cheaply. Often this training was done in secret or in countries where there was no concern about how animals are treated.

SASHA

ONE SERIES OF TV COMMERCIALS featured a rugged-looking bearded man and a giant Kodiak bear of the kind found in Alaska. Together the man and the bear explored the great outdoors. The man paddled a canoe, and the bear swam alongside. The man forded a river clogged with rapids, and the bear walked next to him. The man went fishing and did not catch anything, but the bear caught a fish in its mouth.

At the end of each commercial, the man drank a can of the beer that he and the bear were advertising. As soon as the cameras were turned off, he attached a leash to the bear, then reached into a paper sack and pulled out some candy or dog food for her.

The bear's name was Sasha. When she appeared in the beer commercials, she was two years old and weighed six hundred and fifty pounds. Like most performing animals today, she had never lived as a wild animal.

Sasha was born at the children's zoo in Los Angeles. When she was a few months old, the zoo sold her to an animal trainer in Canada. He sold her to Earl Hammond, the man who trained her for the beer commercials.

Before Earl tried to train Sasha, he watched her for several days. He wanted to learn how she expressed her feelings. What did she mean when she growled or twitched one of her ears or bit on one of her paws? The better Earl understood, the better he would know what her mood was, and the safer he would be.

When Earl first entered Sasha's training pen, he left a collection of treats outside where she could see them but not reach them. There were marshmallows, cookies, jelly, honey, and fruit, all in bear-sized amounts.

Although Sasha was hungry, Earl gave her only a little to eat at a time. That annoyed her, but it helped her to learn that Earl was the person in charge of the food. The sooner she knew that, the better, for only when she did what Earl asked did she get a treat.

Soon he put her on a leash and began training her to walk with him. Each time she did what he asked, he gave her a marshmallow and told her how great she was.

Whenever Sasha saw Earl, she held out a paw for a treat. To encourage him, she would then place the paw on his arm or shoulder. It was pleasant to have her do this, but it was also dangerous. If she ever lost her temper when she was that close, he would have no chance to escape.

Instead of letting Sasha touch him with her paw, he trained her to "kiss" him. He would put out his cheek to her and say, "Give me a kiss, sweetheart." Each time she licked his face without raising her paw, Earl gave her a marshmallow. But whenever she touched him, she got a scolding.

On the days when a commercial was being filmed, usually Earl did not give Sasha any breakfast. He wanted her to look forward to the reward she would get if she behaved.

Earl was never sure that Sasha would do just as she was

told. There always was the chance that she would forget her training and attack him or one of the others who were working with her. "Sasha is not a windup toy," Earl once said. So there was always a gun handy.

The Hustler and the Bears

On a bright, hot afternoon in March 1962, a plane from Holloman Air Force Base in New Mexico landed at Edwards Air Force Base in the Mojave Desert east of Los Angeles. Its only passenger was a 108-pound female black bear in a cage.

The bear was placed in a truck, then driven through the desert heat to an air-conditioned metal building in a remote section of the huge base. An animal keeper removed her from the truck and placed her in a large room with several empty cages.

It was there that she spent the next week, except for a ride in a B-58 bomber and another in an aluminum capsule the shape of a clamshell. She was the first of seven black bears that would take these rides in the months ahead.

The B-58 was the world's first bomber to fly at supersonic speeds. It could climb to 60,000 feet and fly at 1,300 miles an hour, twice the speed of sound. Because the plane flew so fast and climbed so high, the U.S. Air Force had named it the Hustler.

The B-58 had been in use for over a year, but it still did not have a reliable escape system. If the three crew members had to bail out, they were catapulted from the plane by ejection seats, then returned to earth with parachutes.

It was the standard means of escape from a military jet, but the Hustler traveled too high and too fast for the system to work. The lack of oxygen at high altitudes and the violent blast of wind that rushed past the plane made it almost impossible to bail out and survive. As a result, several B-58 crews had been lost.

To solve the problem, the Air Force had developed an escape capsule for the B-58. Instead of bailing out, each member of the crew would leave the plane inside his own capsule. The capsule would be fired from the plane by rockets, then returned to earth by a parachute.

When the bear arrived at Edwards, the Air Force had already begun testing the capsule to decide if it was safe to use. To learn what effects it might have, capsules with living passengers were being fired from a B-58 at different altitudes and speeds.

Along with the seven bears, the passenger list included two chimpanzees and one human being. The bears had been selected because their weight, their spine, and the size of their internal organs were similar to those of humans. The chimps were being used because their nervous system was like that of humans.

At about six o'clock in the morning on March 22, as the sun was rising, several veterinarians arrived to get the bear ready for her flight.

They gave her an injection to put her to sleep during the test. They took samples of her blood and urine to compare with samples they would take after the flight. They fastened electrodes to her head, chest, and legs. These would be attached to a telemetry machine that would send back a report on her heartbeat and her rate of breathing while she was in flight.

At about seven o'clock, they strapped her to a stretcher, then took her to an airstrip two miles away. A B-58 was waiting on the runway. An escape capsule had been installed where the navigator-bombardier usually sat.

The veterinarians lifted her into the capsule, strapped her into the safety harness, and tied her legs in place. They attached a telemetry machine to the electrodes on her body. They also strapped an accelerometer to her chest. It would measure the changes in speed during her flight. At about 7:30, they closed and sealed the capsule.

At about 7:45, the B-58 raced down a runway and took off. The test pilot was at the first station. The bear was at the second station, fast asleep. An engineer was at the third station, where the electronic warfare officer usually sat.

The capsule was to be ejected at an altitude of 35,000 feet and a speed of 870 miles an hour. The pilot headed for a position on the bombing range above the base. Meanwhile, the engineer began a countdown, checking each of the operations that led to ejection. By 8:30 he had worked his way through the list. Everything was "go."

As the B-58 ripped through the sky, the engineer threw a switch that started a pair of high-speed movie cameras. They would film the capsule as it left the plane. When he threw another switch, a pair of rockets fired the capsule, and the bear, to a point several hundred feet away.

Then the capsule began to fall toward the desert floor six miles below. It fell for almost two minutes, from 35,000 feet to 15,000 feet. A large parachute then opened and began to lower the capsule the rest of the way.

After seven minutes and forty-nine seconds, the capsule bumped to a stop in the soft sand. When it was opened, the bear had just begun to awaken. A veterinarian briefly exam-

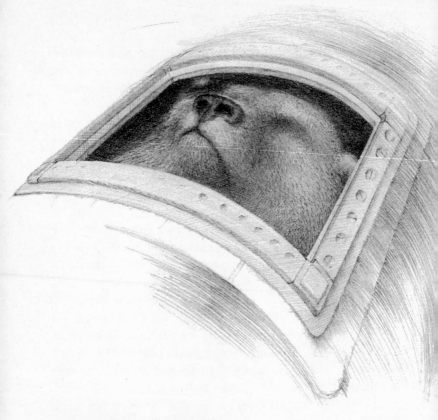

ined her. Then she was placed aboard a helicopter. By 9:30 she was back in her cage.

Over the next few months, six more black bears rode in the capsule. Two of them traveled at 1,300 miles an hour, faster than any bear had ever traveled.

As the bears returned one by one, the veterinarians tried to learn if they had been injured in any way. They put each of them through a series of tests and observed them carefully for several days.

Then they put each of them to death so they could examine their bodies for hidden injuries to the bones and organs. "One-flight bears" was what one of the pilots called them.

As it turned out, only one of the bears had been injured. He was a 178-pound male, the second bear to use the capsule. As it descended, it pitched and rolled and shook violently. The autopsy found that the bear's pelvis, the shield of bone around the lower part of his body, had been broken as he was thrown from side to side in the seat.

When a computer analyzed what had happened on that flight, it found that the pitching and rolling had been caused by the angle at which a rocket had been set. After the angle was changed, the capsule behaved normally.

The testing was completed that summer. In October the Air Force decided that the escape capsule was safe to use. It began to install three capsules in each of the B-58s. It was a decision that seven black bears had helped to make.

NO ORDINARY BEARS

Anyone who has ever seen a bear has a story to tell. But there are bear stories you wonder about. Are they *really* true?

Pete

WHEN I WAS A YOUNG BOY, my father and I were clearing a piece of new land, and out of the woods came a bear cub. It was about as big as a puppy dog. He came right over to me and started whimpering. His mother wasn't around, so after a while I picked him up and took him home. I called him Pete.

I made a pen for him out back and fed him from a bottle. Pretty soon he followed me everywhere. When he got big enough, I started riding him. I just climbed on his back and held on tight. From then on, I rode him whenever I could.

In a few years, I wasn't a boy any more, and Pete wasn't a cub. But I was still riding him. When I started courting, I used to ride him over to my girl's house. Her father wasn't keen on having him around, but Pete minded pretty well. Usually he waited just where I told him to.

One night, I left him behind their lilac bush, but when I came out, he was gone. It was a bright moonlit night, but

I didn't see him anywhere. I figured he had gotten tired of waiting and had gone home.

Then I saw him digging at a stump behind their barn. When I started toward him, he growled at me. He had never done that before, and it made me mad. "He's getting too independent," I thought.

When I got alongside him, he paid no attention. He just kept digging at the stump. When I tried to pull him away, he stood up and gave me a belt in the ribs. When I smacked him back, he took a swipe at me with his paw and ripped my pants. That *really* made me mad, because they were brand-new.

We had quite a tussle, but I finally got him quieted down, and we headed for home. Everything went fine for a while. But when we got within sight of our place, he stopped short and wouldn't move. Well, I lost my patience. I grabbed him by the scruff of his neck and dragged him to his pen. But when I looked inside, there was Pete sound asleep.

A Barrel of Molasses

THERE WAS A FARMER whose molasses kept disappearing. He kept it in a big barrel up in his barn, and it was being used up a lot faster than it should have been.

He figured a bear was taking it. So he made up his mind to catch that bear, no matter what. He waited until the molasses was pretty far down in the barrel, well below the bunghole. (This was the hole he used to draw off the molasses he needed.) Then one night he climbed into the barrel, sat in the molasses, and waited.

Sure enough, in came the bear. He poked his tail through the bunghole, swished it around, and licked off the molasses. Then he tried it again, but this time the farmer grabbed him by the tail, and the bear got scared and started running.

Out of the barn and through a field he ran, with the barrel—and the farmer—bouncing up and down behind him. Then into the woods he went, and on and on he ran. After a while, the barrel started falling apart. First one stave went, and then another and another.

Soon there was only one stave left, the one with the bunghole in it. But the farmer was still holding tight to the bear's tail. Some say he is going yet.

Big As a Cow

The time I'm telling about was eight years ago in November. I helped Bill White butcher his hogs, and he was going to pay me with some of the meat. I hitched my old horse to the wagon and drove four miles through the swamp to pick it up.

By the time I had the meat all loaded, it was getting dark. Bill asked if I had a gun, because there might be some hungry critters along that road at night. I told him I didn't need one. If I moved right along, nothing would bother me.

The first two miles, I got along fine. The moon was shining bright, and the road was out in the open, through cotton patches and cleared fields. But about halfway home, it goes down into the swamp, and it was black as pitch in there.

After a while, I heard this sound. It was like a growl and a grunt. When I looked around, there was the biggest bear I ever saw. He was as big as a cow. He was squatting alongside the road, sniffin' that hog meat, fixin' to jump into the wagon and get it.

I hit the horse a lick with my switch, and he jumped and started moving faster. At the same time the bear jumped. He caught hold of the tailgate and started pulling himself in.

I grabbed a hog's head and threw it into the road, and the bear let go and went after it. But before we had covered fifty yards, he ate up that hog's head and was back.

When he got his nose even with the tailgate, I threw him another piece of meat. He grabbed this one out of the air and swallowed it in one gulp. I threw him some more, but the more he got, the more he wanted.

Then I tied the reins around the footboard and let the horse do his own running. I crawled to the back of the wagon and sat there throwing the rest of the meat to the bear. But I could see that it was just chicken feed to him. When it was gone, he would be ready to eat the horse and me.

Well, the hog meat got lower and lower, and I got more and more scared. When I threw out the last piece, I lay down on the wagon bed and closed my eyes, and waited for the end. But when the bear jumped for the wagon, he missed me. He jumped too far. He went over the tailgate, and over the driver's seat, and landed slap-dab on the horse. Then the wagon stopped moving.

I could hear him up there crackin' and munchin', and I wondered if I should run for it. But I couldn't make up my mind. I just lay there shivering and listening and thinking, when suddenly the wagon started moving again. It was moving faster and faster.

I crawled up to the driver's seat, and there was the bear pulling the wagon along at a gallop. When he ate up the horse, he ate himself right into the harness!

I drove him right on home. By the time we got there, he was gentle as a pony. So I kept him, and I'm still driving him.

The Stump

FROM ALL THE SIGNS, there was a nest of bear cubs some-
where in the neighborhood. Some people wanted to buy a
pair to have as pets. So one day I was putting in some time
trying to find them.

It was pretty warm, and after walking up and down the
ravines, I began to get tired. So I sat down against a big old
chestnut stump about twelve or fourteen feet high. I had not
been there more than a minute when I heard something
inside. It sounded like a couple of bear cubs playing.

I looked all around to find an opening, but there was
none to be seen. Then I noticed claw marks going up the
side of the stump, and I realized that the hole was at the top.
I leaned my gun against a bush, and I climbed up. Soon I
was looking down at two bear cubs the size of small dogs.

I got so excited that I jumped right in. At first the cubs
began to squeal with fright. Then they turned on me, but
they were easy enough to handle. In a minute or two, I had
their mouths tied up so that they couldn't bite, and their feet

fastened so that they couldn't scratch. I knew that the old she-bear would be along pretty soon. So I tied the youngsters on my belt and got ready to get out.

Get out? Did I say "get out"? It makes me shiver just to think of it. I could no more get out of that stump on my own than I could fly. The only way to get out of such a place is to brace your back against one side, and your feet against the other, and "crawl" up. But the hollow was so wide at the bottom, there was no way I could do that.

About the time I realized this, I heard the old she-bear climbing up the outside of the stump. With only my hunting knife to defend myself, you can imagine how I felt.

She was no more than a minute in climbing up, but it seemed like a month. When finally she reached the top, she turned around and began slowly backing down into the hollow, tail first.

I felt as if my last hour had come. I began to think about lying down and letting the bear put me out of my misery. Then I had an idea. "Maybe I am not lost yet," I thought.

I drew out my hunting knife and stood on tiptoe. When the bear was six or seven feet from the bottom, I grabbed her tail with my left hand. Then with my right hand I poked at her bottom with my knife. At the same time, I began yelling like a whole tribe of Indians.

What did she do? She shot out of that stump like a bullet out of a gun, with me hanging on for dear life. Before I knew it, we both hit the ground about thirty feet away. The old bear tore off into the brush and disappeared. I was a little bruised here and there, but that was all. The next day, I delivered the cubs to my customers. Got quite a good price.

Captain Smith and
the Polar Bear

CAPTAIN SMITH HAD JUST come up on deck when he saw a polar bear. It was way out on a big sheet of ice on the leeward side of the bay. He ran back to his cabin to get his gun. Then he started rowing across.

When he got to the other side, he climbed up on the ice and started for the bear. He walked for quite a while. Then, to keep the bear from seeing him, he dropped to his hands and knees and started crawling, staying down as low as he could. When he was about fifty yards away, the captain sat up on his knees and got ready to shoot.

It was just then that the bear finally noticed him and began walking slowly toward him. He was so heavy, the ice bent and cracked as he moved, and water came up and covered that part of the ice sheet.

The captain's legs got soaked, but he decided to stay where he was and hold his fire until the bear got closer. When the bear was only about ten yards away, the captain fired at him. He hit the bear in one of his hind legs, and the bear fell to his knees.

But that didn't stop him. He was too angry at having been shot. Growling and roaring, the bear dragged himself toward the captain. Then the captain shot at him again. But now his gun was empty. So he laid down his gun, grabbed his knife, and started to get to his feet.

But to his astonishment, he found that his legs were frozen fast to the ice, from his knees to his toes. So he put down his knife, doubled up his fists, and shouted, "Come on, you varmint. I'm waiting."

The bear kept coming, but he was moving slower and slower. When he was only a few feet away, he stopped moving altogether. Just like the captain, he had frozen fast to the ice.

When the captain saw what had happened, he burst out laughing. He clapped his hands and slapped his thighs and roared with laughter. But the more he laughed, the angrier the bear got. He roared and roared with anger.

Perhaps it was the terrible roaring of the bear. Whatever it was, the ice they were kneeling on broke off from the rest and started drifting out of the bay. There they were, so close that one could reach out and touch the other's nose.

Soon the wind shifted, and their cake of ice went off to sea. At first the wind drove them north. Then it drove them south. But all they saw was water and ice. They began to get hungry, but there wasn't much they could do about that.

After three days, they were still kneeling there looking at one another, and hungrier than ever, when something came flopping up out of the water onto the ice. It was a seal.

There they sat still as starch as the seal walked right up between them. Then—SLURP! It was all over for the seal, and the captain and the bear began to divide it up. But when the bear wasn't watching, the captain cut an extra portion for himself and put it behind him out of the bear's reach.

When the bear realized what the captain had done, he became very upset. He stretched out as far as he could for the extra piece, but when he couldn't reach it, he roared. Then once more he tried to free himself from the ice. But when he couldn't do that, he reared up and roared and roared and pounded his big paws on the ice.

Soon the ice broke apart again. This time it was right between the bear and the captain. Now there they were, each on his own piece of ice. The captain felt so bad about splitting up that he cut off part of the extra meat he had stolen from the bear and threw it over to him. But the bear wouldn't touch it or even look at it. So off they went drifting apart until they couldn't see one another any more.

But the captain was lucky. In a few hours, a fishing boat spotted him. At first they thought he was a mermaid or a sea serpent. But finally they cut him out of the ice and rubbed his legs to get the blood moving again. Of course, it was a long time before they were back to normal.

Nobody knows what happened to the bear. But the captain had nothing but praise for him. "He was a good sort," he said. "I hope everything turned out all right for him."

My Father's Gun

I WAS WALKING ALONG in the woods with my father's old gun when I ran into this grizzly bear. I fired at him, but I missed, and he started after me. I ran to a big fir tree and dropped the gun and climbed the tree. Then the bear tried to climb it, but he couldn't. He was too big and heavy. So he sat around at the bottom and waited.

After about a half hour, he picked up the gun and pointed it at me. There was nothing in it but an empty shell, and when he pulled the trigger, it snapped. When that happened, he looked up at me, and he held out his hand for another shell. Of course, I wouldn't give him one.

BEAR COUNTRY

The bear's earliest ancestor was a small animal that was something like a dog and something like a bear. Scientists gave it the name *Hemicyon*. It lived over thirty million years ago. It was from this dog-bear that the dog, the coyote, the wolf, the raccoon, and the bear may all have descended.

Bears like those we know today have been on earth for over a million years. At one time they roamed the northern world with the mastodon, the saber-toothed tiger, and other creatures that have long since disappeared.

Bears in North America were wiped out during the Ice Age, when ice sheets extended as far south as Ohio and Montana. This was perhaps eighty thousand years ago. They were replaced by bears that migrated from Asia over a land bridge across the Bering Strait. Today bears are found on every continent, except Australia and Africa, living as they always have.

AS SMALL AS A GUINEA PIG

WHEN A BEAR IS BORN, usually it is only seven or eight inches long, and it weighs less than a pound. It is as small as a guinea pig or a squirrel. It has no hair and no teeth, and it cannot see. In its first days, it looks like a ball of white flesh.

At one time, people believed that the bear's mother licked this ball of flesh into the shape of a bear. This is not the case, of course. On its own, the tiny cub grows into one of the largest and most powerful animals on earth, increasing in size five hundred times.

When an American black bear is fully grown, it may weigh from three hundred to six hundred pounds. An Alaskan Kodiak, the largest of the bears, may weigh more than fifteen hundred pounds and stand eight or nine feet tall.

Most bears have massive, barrel-shaped bodies, long forearms, short, thick legs, and just a bump of a tail. But few people are aware of that tail, for it is hidden by a bear's thick, shaggy fur.

Although bears may seem clumsy, some can run as fast

as twenty-five or thirty miles an hour when necessary. In the Southwest and on the Great Plains, grizzly bears were able to overtake American Indians fleeing from them on swift Indian ponies.

Some bears are remarkable swimmers. Polar bears have been seen swimming forty miles from shore with no ice floes in sight where they might rest.

Most bears also climb trees, and polar bears climb the steep sides of icebergs. Hairs growing on the soles of their feet keep them from slipping, just as the rough hairless skin other bears have on their feet helps them to grip a tree trunk. But the largest bears do not climb trees. They are too heavy to do so.

Except for the polar bear, a bear is usually black or brown or some shade of these colors. American black bears are not only black but also brown, red-brown, cinnamon, tan, cream, and other shades.

In the dark, a bear's small eyes glow like live coals. But its eyesight is weak, and so is its hearing. It depends instead on a remarkable sense of smell. A grizzly bear, for example, can detect the scent of a human fourteen hours after that person has moved on.

SIX GROUPS OF BEARS

BLACK BEAR. The American black bear is found from Alaska and Hudson Bay in Canada to central Mexico. The Asiatic black bear extends from Iran east to Vietnam and Taiwan and north to Manchuria and Japan. This black bear is the smaller of the two species. Its breast is marked with a white crescent.

BROWN BEAR. This group includes the grizzly, the Alaskan Kodiak, and the Eurasian brown bear, all of which are related. The grizzly is found in Alaska, northwestern Canada, and some United States national parks. The Kodiak, the largest bear, is found in western Alaska and on Kodiak Island in the Gulf of Alaska. The Eurasian brown bear lives throughout northern Asia. There also are small numbers in the mountainous areas of Europe.

POLAR BEAR. This is *Ursus maritimus*, the "bear of the sea." It inhabits the land and the ice that border the Arctic Ocean. It is almost as large as the Kodiak.

SLOTH BEAR. A thin, long-limbed, slow-moving animal, the sloth bear lives in the jungles of India and Ceylon. It has long, straight black hair and a yellow crescent on its breast.

SPECTACLED BEAR. This is the only species of bear in South America. It is found in the Andes from Colombia to Chile. It seems "spectacled" because of the ring-like markings around its eyes.

SUN BEAR. This is the smallest of the bears. A full-grown sun bear is about four feet long and rarely weighs over a hundred pounds. Its fur is black and its breast is marked with a white or orange crescent. It is found in Burma, Malaysia, Java, Sumatra, and Borneo.

HOME TERRITORY

MOST OF THE WORLD'S BEARS are "forest bears" that live in wooded or mountainous areas. Through adaptation, others are able to live in canebrakes or swamps, on barren hills, or on desert-like plateaus or frozen tundra.

Bears do not have permanent homes. Instead they travel within a home territory that might be from one hundred to three hundred square miles in size. As they move about their territory, often they follow "bear trails" that were worn in the ground by other bears in the past. They are well-established trails to feeding and watering places.

Usually a bear does not leave its home territory. Only a shortage of food or destruction of its habitat causes it to move elsewhere. Polar bears are an exception to this. As they wander with the drifting ice, sailing on ice floes or swimming from place to place, they cover great distances. In a year, a polar bear may travel a thousand miles or more.

IF YOU COME UPON A BEAR

BEARS ARE SHY ANIMALS. In their travels, they are alone much of the time. They seem to prefer it that way. Even when two bears pass on a narrow trail, or when several feed side by side, they ignore one another.

Bears also try to avoid humans. A person might travel for days through bear country and not see a single bear. Yet bears might be watching silently as he or she goes by.

A bear is not likely to attack a human unless it feels threatened. It may be surprised by someone while eating or sleeping, for example. Or it may believe that its cubs are in danger. Or it may have been wounded or injured and feel that it is cornered.

If you encounter a bear, and you are not armed, an old folk belief advises that you fall down and pretend you are dead. That way the bear will not molest you, it is said. But no one recommends that method today.

Hunters and woodsmen say that you have only a few choices if you meet a bear. One is to stand your ground, behave normally, and not make any sudden movements. If you stay still, the bear may rise up on its hind legs to get a better look at you. Then it is likely to drop to all fours and gallop away.

If you run from a bear, that may encourage it to attack. Yet who would not want to run when faced with an angry bear? If the bear is a big grizzly, your only choice might be to climb a tree, as grizzlies of that size are not likely to do so.

Since no one can predict just how bears will react to a human, the best strategy may be to avoid them. If you are hiking in bear country, wear bells to avoid surprising them. Also try to keep the wind at your back. Any bears down the trail will pick up your scent and are likely to stay out of your way. In addition, try to keep your distance if you see a bear cub, or you may attract its mother.

The grizzly and the Indian sloth bear are regarded as the most ferocious bears. American black bears and Eurasian brown bears are among the most easygoing. These are usually the bears that are trained to perform tricks. Black bears also are talented beggars. They are famous for the food they manage to obtain from campers in campgrounds.

ROOTS, HONEY, AND INSECTS

MOST BEARS ARE VEGETARIANS of a sort. They eat meat and fish, but they prefer fruits, berries, nuts, grasses, roots, honey, and insects. The bear hunter Walter McCracken once saw a grizzly walk into a cloud of yellow-winged butterflies, then rise up on its hind legs and try to catch them one at a time with its forepaws.

With their long curved claws, bears are better equipped to find burrowing insects. But the sloth bear has even more efficient equipment. When it inhales, it can suck insects into its mouth like a vacuum cleaner.

If a bear is hungry enough, it will eat almost anything. It will break into houses, barns, or fishing camps, or wherever else it picks up the scent of food. It will also steal livestock from ranches and farms.

There are many versions of a tale in which a bear races from a farmyard during the night with a live pig in its paws. Usually an old lady in a nightgown is in hot pursuit. She always overtakes the bear and startles him into giving up his prize.

WINTER SLEEP

WITH THE APPROACH OF WINTER, bears in colder climates prepare themselves for their winter sleep. This will help them to deal with the cold and the scarcity of food at that time of the year. Only bears in captivity remain awake. They depend on their keepers to feed them and keep them warm.

The bear's winter sleep is often called "hibernation." But it is not a true hibernation, for the bear's temperature and heartbeat remain near normal. With raccoons, squirrels, and other hibernating animals, the body temperature drops and the heart slows to just a few beats a minute.

In the fall, these bears begin to eat more than in other seasons. The food they do not use up as energy accumulates as a layer of fat. By the beginning of winter, a bear will have acquired several extra inches of fat, as well as a thick coat of fur. When it cannot eat any more, it "dens up."

It digs a hole in a hillside or a riverbank and rakes in dried leaves and grass to lie on. Or it finds a hollow stump or log or a cave high up in a rocky canyon. Or it burrows under the upturned roots of a tree or under some brush and lets the snow build a roof.

A bear's breath and the heat from its body clear away a small "blow hole" in the snow where water vapor and carbon dioxide can escape. The hole is surrounded by a coating of blue ice. To a hunter, this is a sign that there is a bear below.

After a bear settles into its den, it sleeps on and off. Much of the time it may be only half asleep. But it eats or drinks little or nothing. Once it was believed that a bear sucked its paws for nourishment while in its den. This is not the case, of course. It depends on that extra layer of fat for the energy it needs. If the weather turns warm, a bear may leave its den for a while, then return when it gets colder again.

A TIME FOR CUBS

IN JANUARY OR FEBRUARY, while they still are in their dens, she-bears give birth to the cubs they are carrying. A litter may have from one to four cubs, although most often two. After they are born, they remain inside the den with their mother until spring.

It is her job to raise them. She provides their food, teaches them to climb, and protects them. She also gives them a good deal of affection, but she is a stern teacher who will spank them if necessary. Bear cubs usually obey their mothers very well. At just a growl or a grunt from her, they freeze at attention.

Cubs den up with their mother a second time the following winter. Then they are about a year old. But when spring comes, usually they go off on their own. If they don't want to leave, their mother drives them away. Then in May or June she mates again.

THREATS TO SURVIVAL

IF A BEAR IS NOT KILLED by hunters, it may have a long life. Wild bears often live until they are twenty-five or thirty years old. Those in captivity may live even longer.

But there are far fewer bears now than there once were. In the 1870s, for example, there were probably half a million black bears in the United States and over a hundred thousand grizzlies. Today there are only half as many black bears, and the grizzlies are gone, except for a few hundred that are protected in the national parks.

Naturalists are deeply concerned about whether certain families of bears will survive in the years ahead. These include the nine thousand polar bears in the Arctic; the grizzlies in Canada, Alaska, and United States national parks; the few brown bears in Europe; the sloth bears in India; and the sun bears in Malaysia.

One threat to their survival is uncontrolled hunting. At one time, bears were hunted only for the food and pelts people needed. But now they are hunted only for sport, for the thrill that comes with tracking down and killing one of the most powerful animals on earth. Of course, with modern weapons in use, a bear does not stand a chance. Each year in the United States alone, fifteen to twenty thousand bears are killed.

Another threat is the destruction of the habitats where bears live, as humans clear these wild areas for their own uses.

It was these conditions that all but wiped out grizzly bears in the United States. Now other bears may suffer the same fate.

NOTES
SOURCES
BIBLIOGRAPHY

Abbreviations in Notes, Sources, and Bibliography

AA	American Anthropologist
CFQ	California Folklore Quarterly
JAF	Journal of American Folklore
NFA	Northeast Archives of Folklore and Oral History, University of Maine, Orono, Maine
NYFQ	New York Folklore Quarterly
PTFS	Publication of Texas Folklore Society
SDFML	Standard Dictionary of Folklore, Mythology, and Legend
SFQ	Southern Folklore Quarterly
TFSB	Tennessee Folklore Society Bulletin

Notes

For the publications cited, see the Bibliography.

Meat, Fat, and Fur (page 31). People who lived under pioneer conditions depended on bears and other wild animals to meet many of their needs. When they killed a bear, it supplied meat for several weeks or months.

There would be bear steaks, bear hams, bear bacon, bear sausage, even bear's paws, which were regarded as delicacies. Some might even bake the bear's head, a dish "as splendid as it is strange," according to one trapper.

Most people got their bear meat by shooting a bear. In some areas, bear meat was also offered for sale. In Tennessee, in 1787, a hundred pounds of black bear meat, without the bone, sold for eight dollars. In California, in 1850, grizzly bear meat was from fifty cents to a dollar a pound.

"Bear oil" was an important by-product. It was rendered from bear fat, or "bear grease," as it was known. A black bear of average size might yield as much as ten gallons of bear oil.

In cooking, bear oil was a substitute for butter and olive oil. Some said its flavor was superior to that of butter. It was also mixed with sugar and spread on bread. In addition, it was used as a hair dressing, a tonic to cure baldness, and a cure for rheumatism and aching muscles.

A bearskin was usually turned into a rug, a blanket, or warm clothing. See Read, pp. 198–200; Ashton, p. 106; Storer and Tevis, pp. 187–93.

"The Bear in the Sky" (page 33). This legend was told by many Indian tribes in North America. In one version, there are three hunters who pursue the bear. In another version, there are seven hunters involved. The four additional hunters are represented by stars in the constellation Boötes, the Herdsman.

Which version of the legend was used depended on where it was being told. The version with seven hunters was usually given only in the area between the fortieth and fiftieth latitudes, north. In eastern North America, this would be from southern Pennsylvania to northern Newfoundland. It is only in that area that Boötes and its four hunters can be seen in the night sky.

The legend also differs in its details from tribe to tribe. In a version used by the Micmac Indians of Nova Scotia, the seven hunters are birds. In a Blackfoot version from the western United States, the seven are brothers. See Hagar, pp. 95–101.

Ursa Major (page 33). Ursa Major is one of the best-known constellations in the northern sky, for its brightest stars make up the Big Dipper.

North American Indians and ancient Greeks both knew the constellation as the "bear," although neither knew that the others used that name. The Indians called it a bear because the stars that make up the bowl of the Dipper looked to them like a bear. The Greeks called it a bear because of the myth of Callisto and Artemis. Artemis was the goddess of wildlife in the Greek religion. She was the daughter of Zeus, the supreme Greek god. Callisto was one of the young nymphs who served Artemis.

Callisto fell in love with Zeus and with him had a son named Arcas. When Artemis learned of this, she flew into a rage. "I will turn you into a bear!" she shouted. As Callisto wept, fur began to cover her body, and her hands changed to paws. When she tried to plead for mercy, she lost the power to speak. All she could do was growl and grunt. Artemis then banished her to the forests.

One day in her life as a bear, Callisto saw a hunter coming toward her. It was Arcas, her son. She was so glad to see him that she forgot she was a bear. She ran toward him and called his name. But her words sounded to him only like the growls and grunts of a bear. As she approached, he raised his spear to kill her.

At that moment, Zeus intervened. He turned Callisto and Arcas into stars. Callisto became Ursa Major, the Great Bear. Arcas became Arcturus, the Bear Keeper, one of the brightest stars in the sky and close enough to the Great Bear that he could protect her. See Hagar, pp. 92–103; Newell, pp. 147–49.

Before Guns (page 33). Before the development of modern weapons, bear hunters depended on the spear and the bow and arrow, and a number of seemingly simple techniques.

Bears were trapped in deep pits. These were dug near fruit trees or a "honey" tree to which a bear might be attracted. Sharpened stakes were positioned at the bottom of the pit. Then the opening was covered with brush.

If a hunter found a tree limb that led to a beehive, he

sawed halfway through the limb to weaken it. Then he dug a pit under the limb to catch any bears he fooled.

A team of hunters would drive a bear from its den, then try to catch it in a large net or noose. When they caught a bear, they pinned it to the ground with large wooden forks they placed over its legs and throat. If the bear was to be used in a bear bait, they bound it and caged it.

Trip bows loaded with arrows were set up in berry patches where bears fed. If a bear moved the line attached to a bow, the arrows were fired. Trip bows were similar to the spring guns described in the story "The Bear Trap" (page 59).

A weighted trap was used to catch a bear. It consisted of a post to which a heavy movable beam was attached. A piece of meat was hung from the beam by a rope. When a bear reached for the meat, the beam crashed down on top of it.

Dogs were used to hunt bears, as they are today. But in Siberia, perhaps in the fourteenth or fifteenth century, one of the Grand Khans, the leader of the Mongols, trained leopards to find bears for him. See Ashton, pp. 119–23; Jennison, pp. 198–99.

"The Bear Hunt" and Other Lincoln Poems (page 43). "The Bear Hunt" was one of three poems Abraham Lincoln is known to have written. All deal with experiences from the years in which he grew up in southern Indiana. Lincoln shared his poems with a friend, Andrew Johnston, of Richmond, Virginia.

His first poem was written in 1844. It describes his feelings on returning to the place where he was raised. The second was sent to Johnston in September 1846. It tells of a former schoolmate of Lincoln's, who had been insane for the past twenty years.

The last of Lincoln's poems, and the first with a title, was "The Bear Hunt." It also was the first to be published. It appeared in *The Atlantic Monthly* in February 1925. See Lincoln, pp. 277–79; Nicolay, pp. 85–88.

Bear Worship (page 50). Along with American Indians, there are several peoples in the far north who regard the bear as a sacred animal. They include Ob-Ugrians and Gilyaks in Siberia, the Ainu in northern Japan, and the Central Eskimos in Alaska and Canada.

The Ob-Ugrians believe that the bear is a son of Numi-torem, the god of heaven in their religion. Other groups regard the bear as a spirit with impressive powers. It understands humans when they speak. It communicates with God. In some situations, it cures illness.

Because bears are sacred, there are complicated rituals for hunting and killing them, similar to those used by American Indian tribes.

Two groups still sacrifice bears. Each winter the Ainu sacrifice a Himalayan black bear. They raise a bear cub with the same care and affection that they give a child. Then they hold a feast in its honor and kill it. The Ainu believe this frees the spirit of the bear, which enables it to protect Ainu communities from misfortune.

The Gilyak people also sacrifice a bear each year. They believe its spirit will serve as a messenger to God, telling Him of their needs.

See "Bear Cult" and related articles, Leach, pp. 124–27; Cushing, pp. 146–59; Hallowell, pp. 2–175.

The Smithsonian (page 65). The "Smithsonian Institute" on Old Ephraim's grave marker is known officially as the Smithsonian Institution.

Grizzly Adam's Real Name (page 73). Grizzly Adams gave his real name as James Capen Adams, but some scholars believe his name actually was John Adams. According to Adams family records, there were two brothers in Grizzly's generation. One was James Capen; the other was John.

Grizzly died October 25 or October 28, 1860—which date is not certain—and was buried at Charlton, Massachusetts. A tombstone there carries the name "John Adams" and the date of death as October 25, 1860. There also are two references on the tombstone to hunting, an illustration of a hunter and a bear, and an inscription that begins: "And silent now the hunter lays . . ." See Farquhar, as quoted in Storer and Tevis, pp. 217–32.

"*Sasha*" (page 102). Sasha was actually a male bear. But her trainer, Earl Hammond, preferred to think of the bear as a female. If he thought of Sasha as a male, and the bear misbehaved, he might strike him or challenge him in some other way. But, thinking of Sasha as a female, he tended to have the same attitudes toward "her" as he would have toward a woman. He would never think of striking a woman. He would try to coax her to change her behavior. See Hammond, pp. 115–17.

Sasha's commercials were for Hamm's Beer, a Minnesota firm. They were shown in the early 1970s in the South, the Middle West, and the Far West, the regions where that beer was sold.

The first commercials are described in the text. They were filmed in northern California. Sasha and Hammond flew to California from New Jersey. Sasha traveled in a cage in the baggage compartment.

The second series of commercials was about a pack trip Hammond took with Sasha at his side. These were filmed in Minnesota. A third series was about ecology. Hammond helped young people with projects such as planting trees and cleaning streams of debris. These commercials were filmed in

Georgia. Hammond drove Sasha from New Jersey to both Minnesota and Georgia in a trailer. See Hammond, pp. 141–61, 174–94, 222–39.

"The Hustler and the Bears" (page 105). When the U.S. Air Force used seven bears in 1962 in testing the B-58 escape capsule, it made certain that they received humane treatment.

But the Air Force was concerned that the public might learn that the bears were being used as subjects, then losing their lives in the autopsies that followed. Although the use of the bears was not secret, persons who worked on the test recall being asked to "play it down."

When the story was researched for this book twenty years later, the Air Force cooperated. It turned out, however, that a complete record was not available of the role the bears had played.

The author was then put in touch with two persons who had worked on the project, and from there the trail led to others. But their memories of events twenty years in the past were not always in agreement. In addition, the veterinarian who had charge of the bears in 1962 refused to be interviewed. "The use of the bears was a matter of some sensitivity," he said, and he hung up.

The story was pieced together from a small number of newspaper clippings, an article in a medical journal, and telephone interviews with four of the participants. Where minor details were not available, they were based on inferences by the author. See Clarke, pp. 1089–94; "B-58 Ejects a Bear . . . ," p. 15; "Bear Ejected in Test . . . ," p. 7.

The Bear's Tail (pages 117 and 121). Two of the tall tales, "A Barrel of Molasses" and "The Stump," have as characters bears with long, bushy tails. Without these tails, there would be no tales, for the tail of a real bear is actually just a bump hidden by its thick, shaggy coat.

According to a folktale, the bear had a long, bushy tail at one time, but lost it through trickery. One wintry day, Fox persuaded Bear to go fishing through a hole in the ice, and to use his tail as a fishing line. But Bear's tail soon froze fast in the ice, and when he was attacked by some humans and had to flee, his tail broke off.

This tale probably originated in northern Germany about a thousand years ago. It is one of the best-known animal stories in Europe. There also are versions in North America and Africa. But in the African version there is no ice. When the bear places his tail in the water, something bites it off. See "Bear Fishes Through Ice with Tail," *SDFML*, p. 126; Puckett, p. 36; *NYFQ* 4, pp. 112–13.

Sources

The source of each item is given. With folklore, the names of informants (I) and collectors (C) are given when available. Publications cited are described in the Bibliography.

Strange Encounters

p. 11. "In the Dead of Night." McClintock, pp. 103–6. Abridged and retold.

p. 14. "Face to Face." Retold from James Clyman, *American Frontiersman (1791–1881)*, as quoted in McCracken, pp. 116–17.

p. 17. "A Pot of Beans." Retold from Cole, pp. 69–78. For a variant in which a bear enters the house through the floor, see Ferrell, pp. 7–11.

p. 19. "Uncle Lemmie Rassles a Stranger." Meader, pp. 122–24. A Meader family anecdote from Vermont told for generations. Adapted.

p. 21. "Don't Rile Him None." Abridged and retold from Dufresne, pp. 218–23.

p. 24. "Rich, Warm Milk." A New England legend retold from Poole, pp. 366–67.

p. 25. "A Day of Mourning." Based on articles in the Trenton *Times*, Trenton, N.J., June 21–28, 1980.

p. 27. "He Decided to Go Down Fighting." One of several similar New England tales that ridicule the fear some settlers had of meeting a bear. Retold from *Historical Sketches of the Town of Troy, N.H.*, pp. 158–59, as quoted in Dorson, "Just B'ars," pp. 177–78.

Natural Enemies

p. 33. "The Bear in the Sky." Adapted from a Micmac Indian legend in Hagar, pp. 92–103.

p. 37. "Signs." Retold from Laut, p. 629.

p. 39. "In the Deer Yard." Verplanck, pp. 227–40. Abridged and retold.

p. 43. "The Bear Hunt." Lincoln, pp. 277–79. In verse 8, "fice" has been changed to "mutt." The six concluding stanzas, which have been omitted, discuss which of the hunters is to get the bearskin.

p. 46. "The Big Bear of Arkansas." A classic American tall tale, 1845. Abridged and retold from Thorpe, as quoted in Meine, pp. 17–21.

p. 50. "Grandfather, Please Forgive Us . . ." Based on Hallowell, p. 2–175, and "Bear" and related articles, *SDFML*, pp. 124–27.

Outlaw Bears

p. 57. "Old Mose." Retold from Mills, pp. 155–56.

p. 59. "The Bear Trap." Retold from Mills, pp. 157–60.

p. 63. "Frank Clark Kills Old Ephraim." Abridged and retold from Clark, "The Killing of Old Ephraim," pp. 4–5. This story has been written many times, including one version that was included in *The Best Short Stories of 1951*. That one was "The Last of the Grizzly Bears," by Ray B. West, Jr. But Frank Clark, the man who killed Old Ephraim, felt that all the stories about the killing were inaccurate in one way or another. He then wrote the account on which the story in this book is based.

p. 66. "Star Breast." Retold from Dobie, *I'll Tell You a Tale*, pp. 216–19.

Grizzly, Lady, and Ben

p. 73. Abridged and retold from Hittell, 1860 ed., pp. 19–28, 60–61, 104–7, 181–87, 199–205, 268–69, 279, 280, 305–6; 1911 ed., pp. 371–73; Storer and Tevis, pp. 217–38, 244–49; Wright, *The Grizzly Bear*, pp. 112–19.

Captives

p. 91. "Fighting Bears." "Sackerson and Old Nell": References to bearbaiting, *Oxford Companion to World Sports and Games*, pp. 9–11; Conlin, pp. 189–91; Hole, pp. 155–56; the references to Sackerson in *The Merry Wives of Windsor* is from Act I, Scene 1. "General Scott": McCracken, pp. 138–44; Borthwick, as quoted in Haynes, pp. 81–87; fight announcement is slightly abridged. "Bear Fighting": Bell as quoted in Haynes, pp. 75–81.

p. 98. "Performing Bears." "Martin": Vukanic, pp. 106–25; Duff, pp. 129–35; Duffy, p. 58. "Training Bears Today": "Animal Trainers . . . ," *The New York Times*, April 16, 1982; Carson, p. 141; interview with Carmelita Pope, American Humane Association. "Sasha": Retold from Hammond, pp. 110–23, 141–61, 174–94, 222–39.

p. 105. "The Hustler and the Bears." Based largely on the author's interviews with participants in a 1962 United States Air Force research project. Also see Clarke, pp. 1089–94; "B-58 . . . ," *The New York Times*, March 23, 1962, and April 7, 1962. See Notes, "The Hustler and the Bears."

No Ordinary Bears

p. 115. "Pete." Traditional tall tale. NFA: (I) Tom Pond, (C) Mary Lou Dykerman, Frederickton, N.B., 1965. Adapted.

p. 117. "A Barrel of Molasses." Traditional tall tale. NFA: (I) Claire Boulton, (C) Richard C. Wilson, Gardiner, Me., undated. Adapted.

p. 119. "Big As a Cow." Variant of a Munchausen tall tale in which a wolf eats a horse pulling a wagon, then finds itself in the horse's harness and pulls the wagon to St. Petersburg, in *The Surprising Adventures of Baron Munchausen*,

Chap. 3. Retold from Hendricks, pp. 74–77. (I) unidentified truck driver, New Bern, N.C., (C) Mrs. Travis Jordon, Durham, N.C., 1930s. In the version from Hendricks, the bear is driven home, then shot and killed. In a variant, a monster called Old Wall Eyes pursues a wagon filled with meat. See Randolph, *The Devil's Pretty Daughter*, pp. 11–13.

p. 121. "The Stump." Traditional American tall tale. Retold from McClure, pp. 49–50. In a variant, Davy Crockett investigates a hollow sycamore stump, is trapped inside with a bear, then escapes by jabbing the bear's bottom with a knife and hanging on to its tail with his teeth as the bear clambers out. See Dorson, *America in Legend*, pp. 77–79. The folklorist Kenneth Clarke collected an unpublished California variant, "The Big One," in which a hunter is pulled into the sky by ten thousand geese. He is dropped into a hollow stump, where he finds two bear cubs, and escapes with them in the traditional manner.

p. 124. "Captain Smith and the Polar Bear." Retold from Haliburton, pp. 192–202.

p. 127. "My Father's Gun." Retold from Halpert, *CFQ* 4, p. 248; Smith, PTFS 9, pp. 40–43; Harold W. Thompson, pp. 141–42.

Bear Country

The information in this chapter is drawn from books and articles, including Ashton, Cherr, DeGubernatis, East, Gasque, George, Haynes, Krutch, McCracken, Mills, Perry, Storer and Tevis, Van Wormer, and Wright.

The folk belief about playing dead to save oneself from a bear is discussed in "Bear Whispered in Man's Ear," *SDFML*, p. 124.

The reference to a grizzly bear catching butterflies is in McCracken, p. 257. A text of the tale about the old woman who chases a bear that stole her pig is in Speare, pp. 95–96.

Bibliography

BOOKS

Allsopp, Fred W. *Folklore of Romantic Arkansas*, Vol. 2. New York: Grolier Society, 1931.

"Animal-Baiting." *The Oxford Companion to World Sports and Games*. Ed., John Arlott. London: Oxford University Press, 1975.

Ashton, John. *Curious Creatures in Zoology*. New York: Casswell Publishing Co., n.d.

Barnum, P. T. *Struggles and Triumphs; or, Forty Years' Recollections of P. T. Barnum*. Buffalo, N.Y.: Courier Co., 1875. Reprint edition: New York, The Macmillan Company, 1930.

"Bear," "Bear Abductor," "Bear Cult," "Bear Dance," "Bear Fishes Through Ice with Tail," "Bear Medicine," "Bear Wife," "Bear's Son," *Standard Dictionary of Folklore, Mythology, and Legend*, 2d ed. Maria Leach, ed., New York: Funk & Wagnalls, 1972.

Beck, Horace P. *The Folklore of Maine*. Philadelphia: J. B. Lippincott Co., 1957.

Bell, Horace. *Reminiscences of a Ranger; or, Early Times in Southern California.* Los Angeles: Yarnell, Caystile and Mathes, Printers, 1881. Reprint edition: Santa Barbara, California: Wallace Hebberd, Publisher, 1927.

——. *On the Old West Coast, Being Further Reminiscences of a Ranger.* Ed., Lanier Bartlett. New York: William Morrow and Co., 1930.

Boas, Franz D., ed. *The Central Eskimo.* Annual Report of the Bureau of Ethnology. Washington, D.C.: Smithsonian Institution, 1888.

Botkin, B. A., ed. *A Treasury of American Folklore.* New York: Crown Publishers, 1944.

——. *A Treasury of New England Folklore.* New York: Crown Publishers, 1965.

Brown, Charles. *Bear Tales: Wisconsin Narratives of Bears, Wild Hogs, Honey, Lumberjacks and Settlers.* Madison, Wis.: Wisconsin Folklore Society, 1944.

Buffalo Bill [William F. Cody]. *Story of the Wild West and Campfire Chats.* Philadelphia: Historical Publishing Co., 1889.

Camp, Charles L., ed. *James Clyman—American Frontiersman (1792–1881).* San Francisco: California Historical Society, 1928.

Caras, Roger A. *Monarch of Deadman Bay: The Life and Death of a Kodiak Bear.* Boston: Little, Brown & Co., 1969.

Carson, Gerald. *Men, Beasts & Gods.* New York: Charles Scribner's Sons, 1972.

Cherr, Pat. *The Bear in Fact and Fiction.* New York: Harlin Quist, 1967.

Chittenden, Hiram M. *The American Fur Trade of the Far West,* Vol. 2. New York: Press of the Pioneers, 1935.

Chittick, V. L. O., ed. *Ring-tailed Roarers: Tall Tales of the*

American Frontier. Caldwell, Idaho: Caxton Printers, 1941.

Clough, Ben C., ed. *The American Imagination at Work: Tall Tales and Folk Tales*. New York: Alfred A. Knopf, 1947.

Coffin, Tristam Potter, and Henig Cohen. *The Parade of Heroes: Legendary Figures in American Lore*. Garden City, N.Y.: Anchor Press/Doubleday, 1978.

Cole, Harry E. *Baraboo Bear Tales*. Baraboo, Wis.: Baraboo News Publishing Co., 1915.

DeGubernatis, Angelo. *The Animals of the Earth*, Vol. 2. New York: The Macmillan Company, 1872.

Dillon, Richard. *The Legend of Grizzly Adams: California's Greatest Mountain Man*. New York: Coward-McCann, 1966.

Dobie, J. Frank. *I'll Tell You a Tale: An Anthology*. Boston: Little, Brown & Co., 1960.

———. *Tales of Old-Time Texas*. Boston: Little, Brown & Co., 1955.

Dorson, Richard M. *America in Legend: Folklore from the Colonial Period to the Present*. New York: Pantheon Books, 1973.

———, ed. *Davy Crockett, American Comic Legend*. New York: Rockland Editions, 1939.

Duff, Charles. *An Introduction to Gypsies of All Countries*. London: Hamish Hamilton, 1965.

Dufresne, Frank. *No Room for Bears*. New York: Holt, Rinehart and Winston, 1965.

East, Ben. *Bears*. New York: Crown Publishers, 1977.

Farquhar, F. P. "The Grizzly Bear Hunter of California," in *Essays for Henry R. Wagner*. San Francisco: Grabhorn, 1947.

Ferrell, Dorothy M. *Bear Tales and Panther Tracks*. Atlanta: The Appalachian Publisher, 1965.

Gasque, Jim. *Hunting and Fishing in the Great Smokies.* New York: Alfred A. Knopf, 1948.

George, Jean Craighead. *The Moon of the Bears.* New York: Thomas Y. Crowell Co., 1967.

Haliburton, Thomas C. *Traits of American Humor*, Vol. 2. London: Colburn & Co., 1852.

Hammond, Earl and Liz. *Elephants in the Living Room.* New York: Delacorte Press, 1977.

Harrison, Jane E. and Hope Mirrlees. *The Book of the Bear: Being twenty-one tales newly translated from the Russian.* London: The Nonesuch Press, 1926.

Haynes, Bessie D. and Edgar. *The Grizzly Bear: Portraits from Life.* Norman, Okla.: University of Oklahoma Press, 1966.

Hendricks, W. C., ed. *Bundle of Troubles and Other Tarheel Tales.* Writers' Project of the WPA in North Carolina. Durham, N.C.: Duke University Press, 1943.

Hittell, Theodore H. *The Adventures of James Capen Adams, Mountaineer and Grizzly Bear Hunter of California.* San Francisco: Towne and Bacon, 1860; Boston: Nichols, Lee and Cox, 1860. Reprint edition: New York, Charles Scribner's Sons, 1911.

Hole, Christina. *Haunted England.* London: B. T. Batsford, 1950.

Hughes, Langston and Arna Bontemps, eds. *The Book of Negro Folklore.* New York: Dodd, Mead & Co., 1958.

Jennison, George. *Some Curious Chapters of Natural History.* London: A. C. Black, Ltd., 1928.

Johns, James. *The Green Mountain Tradition, or Books of Bears.* Huntington, Vt., 1858.

Kelley, Allen. *Bears I Have Met—and Others.* Philadelphia: Drexel Biddle, 1903.

Kephart, Horace. *Our Southern Highlanders.* New York: The

Macmillan Company, 1927. Reprint edition: Knox-
ville, Tenn., University of Tennessee Press, 1976.

Krott, Peter. *Bears in the Family*. Translated from German
by Ruth Michaelis-Jena. New York: E. P. Dutton &
Co., 1964.

Krutch, Joseph Wood. *The World of Animals: A Treasury of
Folklore, Legend and Literature*. New York: Simon
and Schuster, 1961.

McClintock, Walter. *Old Indian Trails*. Boston: Houghton
Mifflin Co., 1923.

McClure, J. B. *Entertaining Anecdotes from Every Available
Source*. Chicago: Rhodes & McClure, 1879.

McCracken, Harold. *The Bear That Walks Like a Man*. Garden City, N.Y.: Hanover House, 1945.

Masterson, James R. *Tall Tales of Arkansaw*. Boston: Chap-
man & Grimes, 1943.

Meader, Stephen W. *Lumberjack*. New York: Harcourt, Brace
& Co., 1934.

Meine, Franklin J., ed. *Tall Tales from the Southwest*. New
York: Alfred A. Knopf, 1930.

Miller, Joaquin. *True Bear Stories*. Chicago: Rand McNally,
1900.

Mills, Enos A. *The Grizzly—Our Greatest Wild Animal*.
Boston: Houghton Mifflin Co., 1919.

Morey, Walt. *Gentle Ben*. New York: E. P. Dutton & Co.,
1965.

Nicolay, John G. and John Hay, eds. *Abraham Lincoln: Complete Works*, Vol. 1. New York: The Century Co., 1894.

Perry, Richard. *Bears*. New York: Arco Publishing Co., 1970.

Poole, Ernest. *The Great White Hills of New Hampshire*.
Garden City, N.Y.: Doubleday & Company, 1946.

Puckett, Newbell Niles. *Folk Beliefs of the Southern Negro*.
Chapel Hill, N.C.: University of North Carolina Press,
1926.

Randolph, Vance. *We Always Lie to Strangers: Tall Tales from the Ozarks*. New York: Columbia University Press, 1951.

Roberts, Jesse D. *Bears, Bibles and a Boy*. New York: W. W. Norton & Co., 1961.

Sanderson, Ivan T. *Animal Tales: An Anthology of Animal Literature of All Countries*. New York: Alfred A. Knopf, 1946.

Skinner, Charles M. *American Myths and Legends*, Vol. 1. Philadelphia: J. B. Lippincott Co., 1903.

Speare, Eva A., ed. *New Hampshire Folk Tales*, rev. ed. Littleton, N.H.: Courier Printing Co., 1960.

Speck, Frank G. and Jesse Moses. *The Celestial Bear Comes Down to Earth: The Bear Sacrifice Ceremony of the Munsee-Mohican Delaware Indians in Canada as Related by Nekatcik*. Reading, Pa.: Public Museum and Art Gallery, 1945.

Storer, Tracy I. and Lloyd P. Tevis, Jr. *California Grizzly*. Berkeley, Ca.: University of California Press, 1955.

The Surprising Adventures of Baron Munchausen. New York: Pantheon Books, 1969.

Thompson, D. P. *Gaut Gurley or The Trappers of Umbagog*. Boston: John P. Jewett and Co., 1857.

Thompson, Harold W. *Body, Boots & Britches*. Philadelphia: J. B. Lippincott Co., 1940.

Thompson, Stith. *The Folktale*. New York: Holt, Rinehart and Winston, 1946. Reprint edition: Berkeley, Ca., University of California Press, 1977.

Thorpe, Thomas B. "The Big Bear of Arkansas" in Meine, Franklin J., *Tall Tales of the Southwest*. New York: Alfred A. Knopf, 1930.

Van Wormer, Joe. *The World of the Black Bear*. Philadelphia: J. B. Lippincott Co., 1966.

Verplanck, Colvin. *Narrative of a Bear Hunt in the Adiron-*

dacks. Transactions of the Albany Institute, Vol. 6, pp. 227–40. Albany, N.Y.: Joel Munsell, 1870.

Wright, William H. *The Black Bear*. New York: Charles Scribner's Sons, 1910.

——. *The Grizzly Bear: The Narrative of a Hunter-Naturalist, Historic, Scientific, and Adventurous*. New York: Charles Scribner & Son, 1909.

PERIODICALS

Anderson, John Q. "Mike Hooter—The Making of a Myth." *SFQ* 19 (1955): 90–100.

Bankman, Lloyd. "Curt Conklin, the Greatest Trapper." *NYFQ* 22 (1966): 274–97.

Barbeau, Marius. "Bear Mother." *JAF* 59 (1945): 1–12.

"Bear Ejected in Test of B-58 Crew Capsule." *The New York Times*, New York, N.Y., April 7, 1962, p. 7.

"Bears and Bear-Hunting." *Harper's New Monthly Magazine* 11 (1855): 576–607.

"B-58 Ejects a Bear, Animal Parachutes Safely as Craft Hits 870 M.P.H." *The New York Times*, New York, N.Y., March 23, 1962, p. 15.

"Black Bear Is Killed. Meets End in Yardville," related articles. *Trenton Times*, Trenton, N.J., June 18–June 29, 1980.

Clark, Frank. "The Killing of Old Ephraim." *Utah Fish and Game Bulletin* 9 (Sept., 1952): 4–5.

Clarke, Neville. "Biodynamic Response to Supersonic Ejection." *Aerospace Medicine* 34 (Dec., 1963): 1089–94.

Conlin, Matthew. "Bears and Bards: An Adirondack Reverie."

NYFQ 22 (1966): 188–93. A discussion of references to bears in the plays of William Shakespeare.

Cushing, G. F. "The Bear in Ob-Ugrian Folklore." *Folklore* 88 (1977): 146–59.

Dobie, J. Frank. "The Greatest of the Grizzlies." *CFQ* 4 (1944): 12–15.

——. "Storytellers I Have Known." PTFS 30 (1961): 3–29.

Dorson, Richard M. "Just B'ars." *Appalachia* 8 (Dec., 1942): 174–87.

——. "Two City Yarnfests." *CFQ* 5 (1946): 72–82.

Duffy, Marjorie G. "Hot Stove League." *The New York Times*, New York, N.Y., August 9, 1970, Sec. 6, p. 58.

Gibson, Simeon. "Letter to an Ethnologist's Children." *NYFQ* 4 (1948): 109–20.

Hagar, Stansbury. "The Celestial Bear." *JAF* 13 (1900): 92–103.

Hall, Joseph S. "Bear-Hunting Stories from the Great Smokies." *TFSB* 23 (1957): 67–75.

Hallwell, Alfred Irving. "Bear Ceremonialism in the Northern Hemisphere." *AA* 28, new series (1926): 2–175.

Halpert, Herbert. "Montana Cowboy Folk Tales." *CFQ* 4 (1944): 244–54.

Hough, Emerson. "Davy Crockett." *Outing* 42 (1903): 440–48.

Klemesrud, Judy. "Animal Trainers: Unsung Heroes of the Big Top." *The New York Times*, New York, N.Y., April 16, 1982, Sec. C:1, p. 20.

Laut, A. O. "The Story of the Trapper," viii. *Outing* 2 (1903): 628–31.

Lincoln, Abraham. "The Bear Hunt." Charles T. White, ed. *The Atlantic Monthly* 135 (Feb., 1925): 277–79.

Masterson, James R. "Travelers' Tales of Colonial Natural History," *JAF* 59 (1946): 51–67.

Mott, Ed. "When Bruin Wakes." *Outing* 42 (1903): 73–78.

Newell, W. W. "The Bear in Hellenic Astral Mythology." *JAF* 13 (1900): 147–49.

Read, Allen W. "The Bear in American Speech." *American Speech* 10 (1935): 195–202.

Reed, Verner. "The Ute Bear Dance." *AA* 9 (1896): 237–44.

Sloan, Pat. "Slue-Foot, the Indestructible Bear." *West Virginia Folklore* (1966): 16–18.

Smith, Honora D. "Cowboy Lore in Colorado." PTFS 9 (1931): 27–44.

Speck, Frank G. "Penobscot Tales and Religious Beliefs." *JAF* 48 (1935): 1–107.

Stefansson, V. "Icelandic Beast and Bird Lore." *JAF* 19 (1906): 300–8.

Taylor, Archer. *"Schratel und Wasserbar."* *Modern Philology* 17 (1919): 57–76.

Thompson, Harold W. "Tales of the Catskill Bear Hunters." *NYFQ* 5 (1949): 128–33.

Tinsley, Henry G. "Grizzly Bear Lore." *Outing* 41 (1902–3): 154–62.

Vikanovic, T. P. "Gypsy Bear-Leaders in the Balkan Peninsula." *Gypsy Lore* 38, 3d series (1959): 106–25.

Acknowledgments

I am grateful to the following persons for their generous help as I prepared this book:

Professor Edward D. Ives and Joan Warren, Northeast Folklore Archive, University of Maine at Orono; Professor Kenneth Goldstein, University of Pennsylvania; Roland-Évan Rolette; Dr. Joseph L. Hickerson and Gerald Parsons, Folk Song Archive, Library of Congress; Carmelita Pope, Hollywood office, American Humane Association; Lt. Col. Vern Carter of the U.S. Air Force, Fitz Fulton, Robert Sudderth, and Carmie Ziccardi, participants in the B-58 escape capsule project; Lt. Col. Eric W. Solander and J. T. Bear, U.S. Air Force; librarians at Princeton University, University of Pennsylvania, the University of Maine at Orono; the *Trenton (New Jersey) Times*; and Tom Lederer and Joe Sapia, the Princeton (New Jersey) *Packet*.

I also thank Peter H. Schwartz for his bibliographic research and Barbara C. Schwartz for her many efforts in behalf of this book.

A. S.